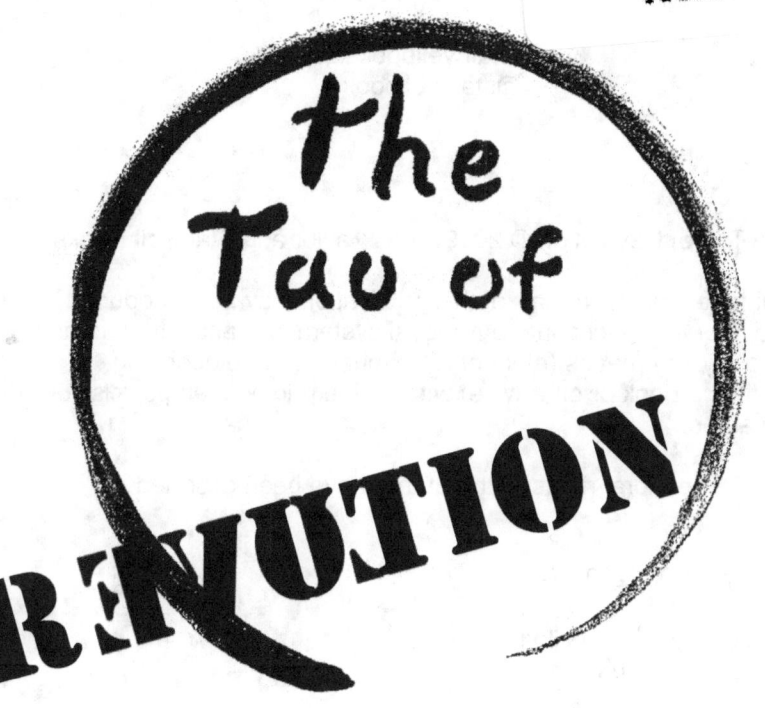

the Tau of REVOLUTION

A field guide to the Global Transformation

or

How to survive the collapse of civilisation as we know it

Chris Taylor

Stairwell Books

Published by Stairwell Books
161 Lowther Street
York, YO31 7LZ

www.stairwellbooks.co.uk
@stairwellbooks

The Tao of Revolution © 2019 Chris Taylor and Stairwell Books

ISBN: 978-1-939269-97-3

Layout design: Alan Gillott
Cover design: Laura Cadman

Dedication

To those

past, present and future,

who decide to give their lives over

to a more beautiful world.

And that probably includes you.

Pay It Forward

Once you have finished with this book, pass it on to someone who might find it of use.

On the other hand, should you want to keep it, encourage your friends to read a copy of their own.
This is another way of living; our lives are too precious to not live them to their fullest and to the greater benefit of the earth which nurtures us.

Contents

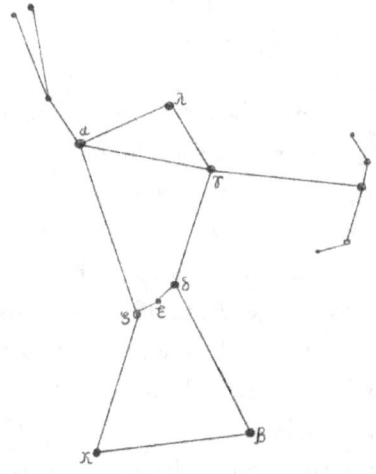

1. The Long Arc

The Long Arc of the Universe bends towards justice. It tugs the stream of events towards right, life, the dynamic equilibrium of disparate elements. But because it is an arc, we can't always tell what's beyond the horizon. In the clatter and cacophony of news-wars, social media bombardments and battling opinions, it can be difficult to hear the low whisper of the future calling.

And the news does not help. In the fear, despair and powerlessness it creates we can come to feel the world is going to shit. Somehow the things we want, or care about, the things that we associate with life, love and happiness seem to be torn to shreds in the remorseless machinations of current events.

Stepping back a bit, it becomes easier to discern the long march of time, the overall direction of history. One realisation is essential: that we are part of the cosmic process, not separate or apart from it. As moves the universe, so moves humanity.

From this perspective the path of the Long Arc[i] becomes clear.

From the primordial soup came simple atoms of hydrogen. From here evolved all the elements of the periodic table, planets, suns, asteroids. All humming to the song of the stars. Then life: microbes, dragonflies, angelfish, dolphins, cats, cows, crows. Hundreds of thousands of species coming and going as the Earth breathes in and exhales across the ages.

The movement of the Universe is from simplicity to complexity. From homogeneity to diversity. From the first faltering building blocks of life to the splendour of a murmuration of starling conjuring sunset against the city skyline.

The evolutionary path is towards conscious self-awareness, a Universe becoming ever more aware of its own existence, its direction, its expansion. A Universe settling into an understanding of eternal rhythm: birth, growth, maturity, death and decay. Then back round again. And again. And again.

In the trenches, amid day-to-day challenges, betrayals and grief, things look messier, more nuanced. There are set-backs, detours, even disasters along the way. At times the human shadow is larger, darker than the light in our hearts. At times despots, psychopaths, dangerous individuals or movements seem in the ascendance. Events do not follow the Arc exactly. Time ebbs and flows in waves, circles back and meanders like an ageless river on an endless plain. But all the while its course is from mountain to sea.

Life is a series of moments, moments that become memories. The patterns that create structure or meaning are not always visible in the moment. They make sense at their deepest level only at the moment of death. Here everything falls into place, making sense, culminating.

The same might be said of the seismic changes shaking the modern world. The patterns and trends will become most apparent once the shift is complete. As we experience them, they can seem random, contradictory, just so much noise.

Which will ultimately be more significant? When we passed 400ppm of atmospheric carbon dioxide or the point where investment in clean energy outstripped investment in fossil fuels? Which will have greater impact on the long-run of history? The rise of authoritarian populism or the tipping point when a majority of the world's population identified itself first as a citizen of the world above citizenship of any one nation?

We are bound by a single market, a single all-consuming consumer culture, an ever-stronger pull into ego mind-set. Will the pull of homogenisation snap us into the embrace of diversity? Will the frenetic noise of materialism awaken us to the still small voice that craves a life of meaning? Or is something else needed to entice us to embrace the global reimagining that stirs beneath the surface of our consciousness?

The truth is, we're in a fix. And we haven't the faintest idea how to get ourselves out of it. In a cataclysmic excess of hubris we have made a grab for control of the most fundamental processes of existence. We brag that we can master the Laws of Nature and rise above all we survey. And then, when we realise too late that we cannot control what we have unleashed, we begin scrambling for survival, at once ashamed of our arrogance and simultaneously in denial that we are to blame.

We have unleashed an unholy fire-storm of rampant materialism, environmental destruction and extreme polarisation. Once this civilisation may have paid tribute to our ingenuity, creativity and productive potential. Now it is a machine beyond our control, a frighteningly destructive force dragging humanity towards its own demise.

And to say it again, at risk of labouring the point, we have no clue at all how to get out of this mess. If we did, we'd have done it. And if we're already doing it and it's just "those others" who aren't, then we still don't know. Because as sure as eggs is eggs, getting out of this will take everyone. Having created a global mega-system, it will take a global response to shift us to a new way of being.

And anyway, the idea that others are to blame, this sense of "us and them", separation from each other, from the rest of nature, from my own life, body, existence, is precisely what got us into this fix. How to get beyond that, globally, is precisely what we don't yet know.

This crisis we have created demands that we face heavy-weight questions: How soon and how severe will the crisis be? Are we on the brink of collapse of civilisation as we know it? Will humanity survive the coming environmental storm? Will life on Earth survive? Is there anything, anything at all we can do to avert it or to ride it out?

3

These are not hypothetical questions. They do not spring from academic interest or a vague curiosity. These existential questions have dogged me for three and a half decades; our global crises demand answers.

I read essays by futurists, looked at climate predications, explored economic scenarios for the next fifty years and delved into the data on resources use and "Peak Everything". These things gave me part of the picture. They did a good job of extrapolating current trends and patterns. They gave me insights into where the current system was heading. Everything pointed in the same direction: global collapse, economic, social and environmental crisis. And it was not far off. There was even a time when the several crises looked like they could collide.

But somewhere along the line I grew tired of directing my energy towards the problems of the world. I lost interest in reading books that told me what was wrong, with only a few pages at the end pointing towards a different way.

My heart began to thirst for a taste of another world. What would it feel like to live there? How would we make a living, organise ourselves, make decisions? Could we possibly create this from the ruins of our current civilisation? So I set out on a quest to understand what is coming towards us.

I needed another way to explore the existential void facing humanity. Something more than science, that had an ancient wisdom. Something that understood the Long Arc of The Universe, that understood the 95% of the Universe that is not matter and therefore cannot be understood by science and rationality alone.

The answer came in the form of the I Ching, the ancient Chinese Book of Changes. The I Ching is a timeless text that documents 64 different approaches to questions of substance. Within its pages I found glimpses of the future echoing back through time and space. This book contains these echoes, the imprecise reverberations of a human future that's ours to create. Each chapter starts with a question with no ready answer. It contains a response from the I Ching and explores the future that is yearning to reveal itself from beyond the Arc of Time.

4

A River in Time

I am blessed to live in the woods, a beautiful place called Rose Valley, with a swift creek passing through all day and night long. Recently, as I sat on the bank aware of her unbroken song, yet empty of thought, I touched the icy water with my foot.

A spontaneous realization rose up in me. I was touching the entire river in that moment – from her origin as a tiny rivulet of rain high in the mountains, to her ultimate surrender to the sea – and every moment along her way. The river begins and ends in the same moment, and transforms again to rain.

I realized that we are like the river. We already are what we seek to become. We have already awakened. We have already transformed. When we deeply touch the present moment, we can remember this.

Rhonda Fabian, Editor Kosmos Journal[ii]

Unanswerable Questions

The road to Lyn Birkbeck's house is not an easy one. His crumbling old home, once proud and lavish sits on a small plot of ground, hidden amongst trees on the edge of a gorge in a small town in the English Lake District. It's damp, shaded and not easy to find, even with GPS.

The first year I visited Lyn, with a good friend, we crossed the stone bridge over the gorge on foot, leaving our cars at the back of a run-down industrial estate. By the second year, the bridge had been washed away in a storm and the only other access was around the other side of town, through a farm yard and down an unpaved track.

What had started as a curious and slightly embarrassing foray into the unknown had become an annual pilgrimage to one of the UK's foremost future-seers. We went first as a bit of a laugh, on the recommendation of colleagues to see if Lyn could tell us anything we didn't already know about ourselves. Over the decades Lyn has filled his house, and his life with a bewildering array of tools to discern the unknowable. Mayan oracles, Tarot and multiple other card sets, runes, star charts. He's got the lot. And he knows how to use them.

The rational science-based thinker in me was sceptical. I have had my fortune told before and it was nonsense. Complete gibberish and guess-work. But this was different. Lyn is no cheap fairground side show. Over the years he has honed a discerning and forensic intuition. What he does is less to predict your future and more to discern the subtle and contradictory forces that are at play in your psyche.

My friend and I were both, in different ways, rocked by his ability to see into the deepest reaches of our souls and pick out our destinies. He certainly saw what made me tick – on both the conscious and sub-conscious levels.

He saw that I had a deep unfulfilled desire for a more meaningful life and a more profound connection with the Oneness of all existence. He spotted the embryonic mystic hiding in my shadows and would have none of my embarrassment or disavowal. And he could see my strong desire to read the future of the human journey.

"Do you use any kind of oracle?" he asked me, as matter of fact as if he was asking what toothpaste I used. I shook my head, not wanting to speak in case I scoffed accidentally. "I think the I Ching would be a very good fit for you."

The I Ching is said to be amongst the oldest texts known to humanity. Its origins are shrouded in mystery. The book is believed to have its birth in the China of over five thousand years ago – before China itself even existed. Before the written word, it is thought a pre-historic chieftain named Fu Xi formulated the sixty-four characters, possibly as an early form of communication[iii].

Fu Xi appears as both a real and a mythical being. As a mythical creature he was half-human, half-snake who, with his twin sister, Nu Wa, created the human race from clay. As a historical figure he is believed to be the first male chieftain to take power as early Chinese society moved from a matriarchal community (where Nu Wa was a powerful influence) to a patriarchal society. Fu Xi is credited as the inventor of hunting, fishing and cooking.

This is described in the classic text, Baihi Tongyi:

> *In the beginning there was as yet no moral or social order. Men knew their mothers only, not their fathers. When hungry, they searched for food; when satisfied, they threw away the remnants. They devoured their food hide and hair, drank the blood, and clad themselves in skins and rushes. Then came Fu Xi and looked upward and contemplated the images in the heavens, and looked downward and contemplated the occurrences on earth. He united man and wife, regulated the five stages of change, and laid down the laws of humanity. He devised the eight trigrams, in order to gain mastery over the world.[iv]*

Two millennia later, the founders of the Zhou Dynasty, King Wen and his son the Duke of Zhou are said to have collected or composed sayings attached to each of the characters. King Wen is also said to have put the sixty-four hexagrams into their current order while he was imprisoned by the King of Shang during the Warring States period.

Later still, around the fifth or sixth century BCE, Confucius is thought to have refined the text of the I Ching – either directly himself or via his students and followers. At around this time a band of philosophers emerged who felt society had lost its old ways so they set out to elucidate The Way (The Tao) to live in harmony with the flow of events. A later Chinese scholar, Ch'eng I of the eleventh century, puts it this way:

> *"The word I of I Ching means change; that is, changing in accord with the time so as to follow the Tao. As a book, the I Ching is vast and comprehensive: by following the principles of essence and life, understanding the reasons of the obscure and the obvious, and comprehending the conditions of things and being, it shows the way to enlighten people and accomplish tasks."*[v]

It is believed that there are forces operating, waves of change in human life, in nature, in the fabric of the cosmos. If we understand these movements we can appreciate the most productive way to act – or indeed not to act at all, until the time is right.

Amongst the first Westerners to study the I Ching was psychologist Carl Jung, who had a penchant for combining the scientific with the mystical. He was fascinated by the more intangible aspects of the human experience.

In his Foreword to an early translation of the I Ching, Jung writes:

> *In order to understand what such a book is all about, it is imperative to cast off certain prejudices of the Western mind... Our science is based upon the principle of causality... If we leave things to nature, we see a very different picture: every process is partially or totally interfered with by chance, so much so that under natural circumstances a course of events absolutely conforming to specific laws is almost an exception.*[vi]

Over the past five years the I Ching has become a tool for me. When I face a situation or a challenge that seems to have no easy answer, no obvious solution, I turn to the I Ching for a new perspective. How might I approach this conundrum in a way that is productive? When the science of the 5% reaches its limits and rationality has been all the assistance it can be, I turn to the intuitive wisdom of the 95% for guidance.

I decided that this approach is worth a try. At times I'm prepared to go with science and rationality. At others I'll go with poetry, pattern, omen and signs.

The human experience is both material and mystical. In truth, both are interwoven. The fabric of the Universe and that of the human reflect each other in wonderful coincidence. As modern Taoist Master, Professor Huai-Chin Nan reminds us:

> *"According to modern medicine, the mean normal respiration rate is 18 times a minute. The normal mean pulse rate is 72 times a minute, four times the respiration rate. An average man's respiration rate adds up to 25,920 times a day – exactly the same number as the number of years in a Great Sidereal Year. A Great Sidereal Year is the length of time it requires for all the planets in the solar system to return to their original positions."[vii]*

Our natural rhythm of life is truly in harmony with the movements of the universe we inhabit. How could it not be?

This book then, is 5% science and 95% intuition, conjecture, mysticism. It draws as much upon the ancient oracle of China, The I Ching, as upon the latest texts on economy, sociology, globalisation. I have lived in both worlds, studied both. I have come to trust my intuition – provided I can distinguish it from pride, prejudice or pomposity.

These pages are the intuitive discernment of what's to come, gathered from what I've learnt and from the hearts and souls of people I have met from across the world: people sensing their own way into creating the new story of human evolution. People who are writing a new and ancient story of how to live in balance with a miraculously abundant planet[viii].

The people who fill these pages are precious individuals I have met as I wander through the movements, alliances and collectives who are doing everything in their power to build the world they want their children to inhabit. Some are friends, some acquaintances, a few are people who I have read but never met. All are folk who have touched my life, given me insights or inspiration. They have become travelling companions on the journey into the future of humankind.

Each section of this book contains a Reading from the I Ching which I took to answer the unknowable questions that were dogging my dark nights. The answers often surprised or confused me. They did not match my received wisdom of social change, progress, economic development. They often questioned the arrogance of my view of human civilisation, technology and growth. In the end they made me question the very foundation of my own life, what gave it meaning and where it was heading.

They were seldom comfortable reading but I took them seriously, even when they didn't align with my preconceptions or established world-view. Following their lead took me to places I did not expect to go, to conclusions that changed my outlook and even the course of my life.

Dissolution

When your soul calls from further down the road,
turn. Run to meet it.
There will be time enough to dawdle
in your twilight years.

When the voice of doubt pinches your toes
like last year's shoes,
thank it for its kind concern
then do it anyway.

And when fear boxes you in at every turn
know that its purpose is to be the maze
that guides you to the place
where life dissolves into a world at one.

2. Now Underway

What is the Nature of this Moment in History?[ix]

You must go through a transformation that is beyond your control. In the end it will reveal your hidden potential and open a whole new field of activity...

This is now underway but you can do nothing about it. Trying to impose order or to leave the situation would close the way.

This transformation reveals a deep, perhaps unacknowledged need. Be receptive and adaptable. Act through the woman and the yin.

This process is both an end and a new beginning. If Heaven and Earth did not mingle like this, the myriad things would never emerge.

Look at things from an independent perspective. If you stay in the shade, hidden and secure, this will bring profit and insight.

The accepted time has gone by. Let it go. Draw things out. This procrastination will lead to the right time to act. A significant connection is approaching.

This is a time of rebirth and returning energy after a difficult time... Return to the source. Restore the original purity and feeling... Stir things up and go with the movement. Let things emerge without pressure. Heaven is moving here. In returning you see the heart of Heaven and Earth.

[I Ching 54, Converting the Maiden; transforming to 24, Returning]

The Accepted Time

In the eye of the storm, when the transformation is well and truly underway, there is a point where it is impossible to know what to do. Nothing that has worked up to that point is of any use. As Einstein famously said you cannot use the same thinking that got you into the situation. What may have served you in the past, the status quo and its mind-set, become a hindrance.

The only thing to do is to let go and see what arises. This is the age old practice of allowing emergence. In a world full of noise, action and motion, how much do we remember about working with emergence? When our models of leadership promote decisive action, strategic direction and powering through adversity at all costs, are we really preparing ourselves to deal with complexity, uncertainty and not-knowing?

The point of no return has passed and we are heading into the storm of global transformation: the death of one system and the birth of another. The signs are all around us:

> *In The Age of Decadence... everyone is focussed on their self-interest. Elites protect their wealth, leaders protect their power and the masses clamour for entertainment. We worship actors, musicians and athletes. We are bought off with food and grand spectacles; we become obsessed with sports...*
>
> *I know this sounds depressingly familiar, so let me remind you that this is how humans always behave during the decline of their civilisation. Always.*[x]

These are the words of Margaret Wheatley, complexity scientist and veteran community activist. The prophets of capitalism call this the End of History, trying to persuade themselves that we have attained a higher state of human civilisation. In truth we are repeating the age old cycle moving from simplicity to complexity to collapse. And then back round again. At the point of highest complexity we descend into decadence.

We have surpassed every known barrier to our own existence. Our water is full of poisons from our factories and fields. The food we eat has more chemical than nutritional content. The soil it is grown in barely has enough nutrients to survive; it is virtually dead. The air is so full of pollutants that the very atmosphere has changed its composition, pushing the climate into chaos along the way.

Humankind could be the only species ever to subconsciously cause its own demise. We seem to have a suicidal death wish. Ecological boundaries fall with every new climate report. Economically too we are heading for disaster. The booms and busts of the past are ignored as we tank ever onward fuelled by adrenaline, greed and a maniacal sense of insecurity that drives us to accumulate way beyond necessity.

And there is very little any of us can do about it. World leaders swarm into global summits and agree business as usual. The most conscious citizens attempt environmental lifestyles but end up relying on technologies (hybrid cars, photovoltaic cells) which have such heavy footprints built into their production they will never be offset by use.

Whatever we do seems to make matters worse. We are past the point of no return. The Accepted Time has passed. We must now see this out. It is an end and a new beginning. But you cannot begin until the old has seen itself out the door.

Gaia, the spirit of the living planet, has her limits[xi]. She is a complex, living, ever-changing system composed of billions upon billions of inter-dependent, evolving parts. She survives and grows through dynamic equilibrium, the balance, ebb and flow, shifting relationships between parts. If any part falls out of balance, the whole system is in some way impacted.

Each element has its unique role. It is food for another part, it creates waste to nurture something else, it breathes in someone else's out-breath. The Whole requires balance, within the bounds of complex interdependencies.

While everything is of equal value and worth, a group of inquirers at Stockholm Resilience Centre have suggested that there are nine critical systems that are vital to the continuation of The Whole. We might think of them as the vital organs of a living system.

If we cross one of these Planetary Boundaries it will be hard to set that part of the system back on track. There is a point of no return. If we cross too many of the nine, the system itself may start to disintegrate. Without her vital organs, the capacity of Mother Earth to generate and sustain life will be compromised. Some say it will take one hundred thousand years to recover, by which time humanity could be extinct.

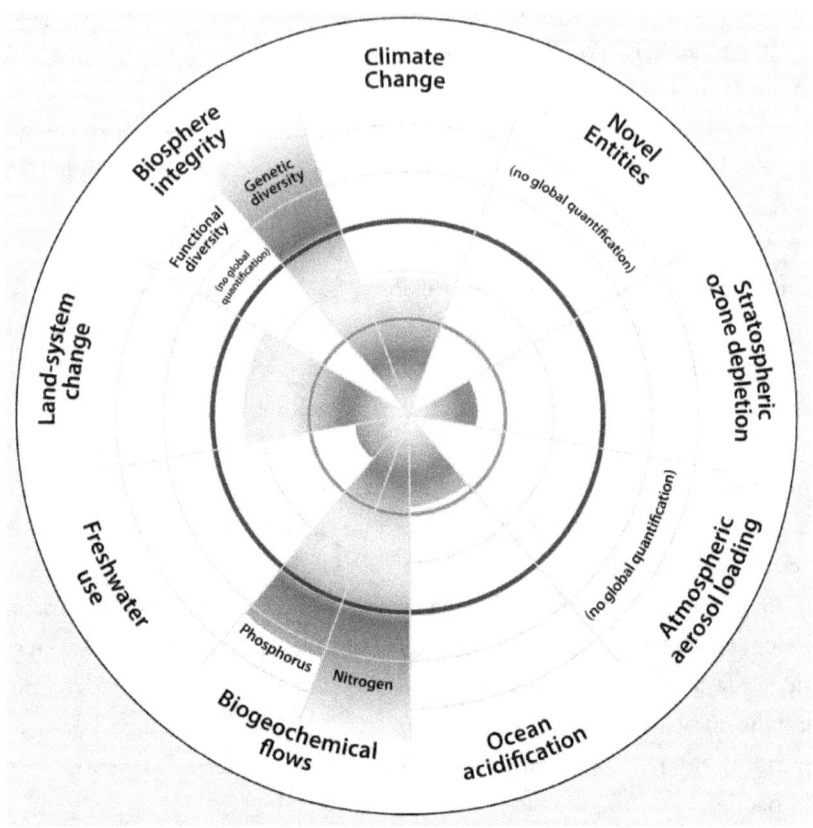

As the climate warms so do the oceans. This changes the pH levels causing acidification which bleaches coral, killing it in boiling acid water. A change in the air causes a change in the water which causes death and decline.

Similarly, overuse of synthetic nitrogen and phosphorous in agriculture washes into the seas causing seasonal dead-zones in coastal waters. And we know water is life. We are pushing it to breaking point. Push too hard and life itself will become precarious, eventually impossible.

The Economy has no regard for such delicate relationships. Capitalism is based on a single dynamic: constant, infinite growth. In nature, things are kept in balance by dynamic interactions like predator and prey. This stops any part of the system growing out of control.

The only thing that doesn't respect this law is cancer, which is growth out of control, with no natural predator. Cancer too is an unnatural phenomenon. And capitalism is cancer in the blood of Gaia.

Over the course of its 500 year history, capitalism has grown from its roots in Europe to swallow up the entire globe. It now reaches into the most remote village in central Africa, the mountain kingdoms of the Himalayas and the plains of the Andes. Its tentacles entangle every aspect of our lives: food, clothing, work, learning, entertainment.

Competition between corporations drives them to maximise their profits and their own growth in order to survive. Some find a way to do this in balance with other factors, such as workers' conditions or by reducing their environmental impact. Others do not. Overall the system operates to prioritise profit at the expense of social and environmental impact.

Built on the pursuit of profit, the entire system feeds on one half of the human soul: competition, fear of scarcity, self-interest, lust and greed. These characteristics are not the only side of human nature. It is just that our survival within a capitalist world market requires that we practice, perfect and employ them in order to succeed.

What were once free goods, fruits and vegetables gathered from the Earth, become commodities bought and sold on global markets. Capitalism survives by taking things that used to be free and making them into a product (or service) to buy and sell. This is the process of commodification that creates profit and drives the spread of the marketplace.

Now we are approaching the limits of this seemingly infinite expansion. The Economy is butting up against the limits of The Ecology. It is starting to breach the ecological systems that bring life to the planet.

At the same time, something else is happening. The ability of the economy to expand is becoming increasingly constrained. Profits are shrinking, growth is slowing and the economy is sluggish in all but a few fast-developing pockets in the Global South.

This impending crisis was first predicted by Karl Marx who in the course of his writings identified a range of ways in which capitalism was socially, economically and politically unstable. On the economic front, Marx argued that the rate at which the system generates profit would naturally fall – margins would get slimmer and slimmer as time went on. This would make the pursuit of profit ever more frantic until the system collapsed.

In Volume 3 of his magnum opus Das Kapital, Marx arrived at a very simple mathematical formula to describe the way that profits were destined to fall. Basically this suggests that profits decline as the costs of capital (machinery, raw materials etc.) or the costs of labour increase. Simple enough.

I came across this formula in 1985 in my final year of college. It struck me that it demonstrated a fatal flaw in the capitalist economy that few people had noticed: under capitalism the cost of living and by implication the costs of labour, only ever goes up (we call this inflation).

This is because capitalism makes people in its sphere of control dependent on the things it sells them. Food, shelter, education, spaces to meet in to socialise: all require money. The more capitalism expands into our lives, the more it commodifies things that were previously free – childcare, ready meals, health, education. This is essentially the same thing as saying that GDP rises.

In this way, capitalism inadvertently makes the costs of employing people more expensive. This in turn means the rate of profit falls. The economy grows, but the margins of companies in it are continually being eroded in percentage terms – forcing them to grow, merge, innovate in order to survive.

To put it all in a nutshell: capitalism survives by constantly extending the market into all corners of life. As more and more aspects of existence are brought into the cash economy, the cost of living rises. This means people need to earn more just to survive and this upward pressure on wages causes the rate of profit to fall. The central dynamic within capitalism constantly and progressively undermines its ultimate survival.

The end can be forestalled by moving production sites to lower wage parts of the world. But this is only a temporary solution because the commodification process happens here too, gradually pushing up wages. So China moved from being the manufacturing zone of choice, because of abundant cheap labour, to being undercut by other venues as it became a consumer society and its wages started to rise.

The system continues to grow until it has colonised the entire globe reaching into all corners of our lives. At that point it will collapse as profits disintegrate, debt cannot be paid and people cannot earn enough to survive.

Marx was pretty clear about this himself:

> *"No social order ever perishes before all the productive forces for which there is room in it have developed; and new higher relations of production never appear before the material conditions of their existence have matured in the womb of the old society itself. Therefore mankind always sets itself only such tasks as it can solve."[xii]*

We should not expect the system to collapse before it has run its course. It is too powerful while it is still expanding, too capable of financing all the tools of persuasion, distraction, repression and division. As with many things, all the best things, so too with revolution: timing is everything.

But collapse it will. The only question is, how close is this collapse and how catastrophic will it be?

Beyond Control

Thursday November 9th 1989 is a chilly autumn night like any number before and since. Yet this is a night that will forever change the face of Europe. Something unexpected, something almost magical happens, seemingly out of nowhere.

Forty years earlier, as the dust settled on a Europe devastated by World War II, the battle-lines were drawn for a Cold War, a continual high stakes game of nuclear chess between power-blocks representing free-market capitalism on the one hand and state-managed socialism on the other. The continent hung under the cloud of a military strategy that promised Mutually Assured Destruction. Peace would be kept by the threat of total and complete annihilation. Two ideologies faced off across a continent.

We lived with a constant background fear that nuclear war could start at any moment – either by accident or deliberately as the two superpowers tried continually to gain dominance over the other. Nowhere was this division more striking than in the city of Berlin. Here a wall had been built dividing the city in halves controlled by the competing empires.

By the late 1980s it was becoming clear to astute observers that the Eastern Bloc was straining under the financial weight of the arms race. The design, production and deployment of arms was driving the Soviet Empire to the brink of bankruptcy. This was clear to political scientists but not as obvious to the general populations on either side of the Berlin Wall.

On the night of 9th November people mysteriously start gathering on the East German side of the Wall. Over recent weeks the state has been granting permission for people to visit family in the West. Now a rumour is going round that a regulation has been passed that any citizen can leave the East by any of the border crossings. In effect, the wall is to be opened.

Soon 2,000 people have gathered at Checkpoint Charlie, the most famous crossing point. What unfolds during the night is a mixture of accident, mishap and miracle. It starts with a hapless East German official misinterpreting a press release from his superiors – and the

Western media jumping to the wrong conclusions. Border Guards, unable to contain the waiting people and failing to get clear orders from their superiors, start to make decisions for themselves. A café owner on the western side takes drinks to the Eastern Guards and on his return is mistaken by journalists for a celebrating Eastern escapee.

At around half past seven in the evening, radio stations excitedly report thousands of people pouring across the border. In fact this is not true and only inflames passions at the crossing gates. In an attempt to calm things at the border, guards are then told to let through the most vocal protesters – in the hope that the rest will be calmer without them.

This backfires, as the crowds see it as a sign that it is possible to leave. And so, by the end of the evening, people are flooding across the border. By 11 o'clock crowds in the West are becoming more and more restless – greeting Easterners with beer, kisses and handshakes. Checkpoint Charlie, the Brandenberg Gate and the Bornholmer Street crossing are all inundated at both sides. Eastern Guards are unable to hold back the crowds and unwilling to fire upon them. They decide instead to open the gates and let people flood through.

Just after midnight people start hacking at the wall with hammers, pick axes, and anything else they can lay their hands on. By morning, sections of the wall have been hauled down by the hands of the throng, while elsewhere easterners and westerners party together through the night, celebrating the collapse of a wall that had divided families for decades: a wall we had all thought to be an immovable part of the landscape.

Like the Berlin Wall, sooner or later all social and economic systems collapse. Be it benign or despotic, no system lasts longer than its internal contradictions can hold together. Our current system is no different. We are approaching the November 9th of global capitalism.

There are many theories about why empires collapse. Historians are captivated by their ebb and flow. What happened to the people who carved the Easter Island Statues? How did the Maya or the Inca come to an end? Weren't there advanced civilisations in Southern and West Africa – what happened to them?

21

Many empires are overrun by warring neighbours. Others fall apart of their own accord. Often this is when natural resources are exploited beyond the local environment's capacity to replace them. This can be exacerbated by climate changes or population growth.

Jared Diamond, who has studied civilization collapses in detail, has identified five factors which usually bring an empire to its knees: environmental damage, climate change, hostile neighbours, relations with trade partners and the society's response to its environmental problems. It is the last of these that usually proves fatal.

In the chapter of his book Collapse entitled "Why Do Some Societies Make Disastrous Decisions?", Diamond lists a whole array of reasons why societies continue a path towards their own destruction. Maybe they don't see it coming, or can't find a solution, or maybe there are vested interests at work. One crucial factor, he postulates, is that elites within the society may be so out of touch with the rest of society that they pursue their own narrow interests with impunity:

> *If the elite can insulate themselves from the consequences of their actions, they are likely to do things that profit themselves, regardless of whether those actions hurt everybody else... Throughout recorded history, actions or inactions by self-absorbed kings, chiefs, and politicians have been a regular cause of societal collapses, including those of the Maya kings, Greenland Norse chiefs, and modern Rwandan politicians.*[xiii]

Another US academic who has studied collapses is Joseph Tainter. His theory is that societies collapse when they become too complex to be governable. Civilisations move in a cycle: from simple to complex, then to collapse and back again to simplicity.

What is different at this point in human history is that the system on the verge of collapse is a global one. This means the change, when it comes, will be global. Jared Diamond spotted this:

> *Globalization makes it impossible for modern societies to collapse in isolation, as did Easter Island and the Greenland Norse in the past. Any society in turmoil today, no matter how remote ... can cause trouble for prosperous societies on other*

continents and is also subject to their influence (whether helpful or destabilizing).

For the first time in history, we face the risk of a global decline. But we also are the first to enjoy the opportunity of learning quickly from developments in societies anywhere else in the world today, and from what has unfolded in societies at any time in the past. xiv

Our world, our entire global civilisation is on the brink of a breakdown – or possibly a breakthrough. This has never happened before. Empires, nations, kingdoms have only ever covered part of the Earth. Now we are bound in a single system. When it collapses, transforming into something else, it will call the whole of humanity to imagine and create what comes next.

The Shambhala Prophecy

There comes a time when all life on Earth is in danger. Great barbarian powers have arisen. Although these powers spend their wealth in preparations to annihilate one another, they have much in common: weapons of unfathomable destructive power, and technologies that lay waste our world. In this era, when the future of sentient life hangs by the frailest of threads, the kingdom of Shambhala emerges.

You cannot go there, for it is not a place; it is not a geopolitical entity. It exists in the hearts and minds of the Shambhala warriors. Nor can you recognize a Shambhala warrior when you see her or him, for they wear no uniforms or insignia, and they carry no banners. They have no barricades on which to climb to threaten the enemy, or behind which they can hide to rest or regroup. They do not even have any home turf. Always they must move on the terrain of the barbarians themselves.

Now the time comes when great courage – moral and physical courage – is required of the Shambhala warriors, for they must go into the very heart of the barbarian power, into the pits and pockets and citadels where the weapons are kept, to dismantle them. To dismantle weapons, in every sense of the word, they must go into the corridors of power where decisions are made.

The Shambhala warriors have the courage to do this because they know that these weapons are manomaya. They are "mind-made." Made by the human mind, they can be unmade by the human mind. They arise from our own decisions, our own lifestyles, and our own relationships.

So in this time, the Shambhala warriors go into training. They train in the use of two weapons. The weapons are compassion and insight.

24

You have to have compassion because it gives you the juice, the power, the passion to move. It means not to be afraid of the pain of the world. Then you can open to it, step forward, act. With that wisdom you know that it is not a battle between "good guys" and "bad guys," because the line between good and evil runs through the landscape of every human heart.

But that weapon by itself is not enough. It can burn you out, so you need insight into the radical interdependence of all phenomena. With insight, you know that actions undertaken with pure intent have repercussions throughout the web of life, beyond what you can measure or discern.

Together these two can sustain us as agents of wholesome change. They are gifts for us to claim now in the healing of our world.

Joanna Macy, Earth Advocate, recounting the words of Tibetan Monk Choegyal Rinpoche[xv]

Letting Come, Letting Go

These are complex times negotiating the final days of the world's greatest empire. We will have to dance between the falling glass and steel, our glance darting upwards, our senses alert as the temples of greed and vanity collapse around our feet.

These are the final days for sure. They will unfold in our lifetime. The signs are all around. As every civilisation reaches its zenith the pace of accumulation hastens. Trinkets are hoarded by the privileged, drunk on their own self-worth.

Demagogues compete to over-perform in the game of puritanism. Celebrity becomes vacuous, culture eats itself. These signs have appeared in all Final Days: watched by the masses before they turn away to something new; ignored by the elite consumed by the drugs of decadence.

There is no telling which crisis will deal the death blow: perhaps the economy – the mountain of debt, the commodification of everything, one final boom-and-bust cycle. Perhaps the ecology – the death of the world's children, the process that turns soil to dust or oceans to acid. Perhaps even the crisis of the human soul – the weight of this destruction might cleave us in pieces, shattering frail hearts, calling us to pain, grief, anger and action.

There's no telling how this will unfold. But unfold it will. These are the final days our ancestors talked of, because they knew them all too well. They had moved through four worlds to get here. Through the rise and fall of empires in deserts, savannahs, continental plains, island paradises. Now we are destined to live it all again, here across the entire face of this fragile orb.

These are complex times negotiating the hopes and fears of the human heart. The tug of the familiar distracts us from letting go and moving on. We cling for dear life to the sinking hull of the Titanic, still convinced it is the greatest ocean-going liner ever built; still unable to come to terms with it disappearing beneath the waves. We laugh and cheer at the string quartet playing while the water laps at their sequinned shoes. Their poise is unsurpassed; the tune vaguely familiar and hauntingly poignant.

There's no telling how this letting go and letting come will play out. It takes divine courage to let go and push out into the darkness of the ocean night. It takes a faith beyond reason to allow civilisation to sink knowing nothing of what will rescue us – nothing except the faintest call from the darkest parts of our frozen hearts.

There's no telling how soon the turning will come, how long it will last. The way of things is faster than we suspect, at the moment we least expect it. But then the rebuilding takes more, digs deeper, calls forth more energy that we thought possible.

Immanuel Wallerstein is the man I trust most on these matters. I first came across his work in library at Sunderland Polytechnic, where I took my first degree. This was back in the 1980s when Sunderland was a city recovering from the demise of its heavy industries, mining, shipbuilding, and facing into the battle for survival.

Wallerstein has studied the world system from its inception in the 15th Century to its impending demise. When I wrote to him asking for guidance, he was confident in his estimation: "For a long time, I have been saying things will run to more or less 2040-2050,"[xvi] he assures me.

I hope he's right. I cannot stand this much longer. It goes against everything I know is true about the human spirit. And still, I'm not sure we're quite ready for what's ahead. Let's steady ourselves. Take a few deep breaths. Straighten our backs, make sure we have fed and watered ourselves in preparation for what's to come. Let's empty our heads, open our hearts, step forward only when ready. We have waited an age for this moment. Let's not waste it in haste.

An End and a New Beginning

It turns out that the completion of the Maya Calendar in 2012 did not bring the end of the world. Maya observers knew it wouldn't – that their ancient calendar had been misinterpreted by some in the Western world.

It was never about the End of Days. It was always more subtle than this. Maya shaman Ohky Simine Forest puts it like this:

> *The majority of ancient prophecies around the world speak of the shifting eras at the end of the twentieth century... All of them refer to a major transition we are about to live, if we are not living it already.*[xvii]

Schooled as a shaman in her own Iroquois tradition, the Maya tradition of her husband and the Mongolian shamanic tradition, Ohky found striking similarities between the three cosmologies and their prophecies of a changing world.

The era that straddles the turning of the millennium is seen as a period of dreaming, envisioning. A period that marks a shift from the masculine era of materialism into a feminine period of community and deeper democracy. Truly a time of Global Presencing[xviii], when the world can reimagine itself from the stillness between stories. It started in the mid 1980s around the time of the fall of the Berlin Wall. It continues now as we dream in clusters, movements, waves of human consciousness, of a More Beautiful World, manifesting what sits still and calm within our hearts.[xix]

Legends tell of this time. In North and Central American there is the Prophecy of the Reunion of the Condor and the Eagle – representing the peoples of the North and South, the union of science and spirituality, the reunification of humanity in a golden age.[xx]

Indian cosmology sees a cycle of Ages, and the world passing back into a Golden Age at about the turn of the Millennium. The Brahma Kumaris, a matriarchal spiritual movement have been preparing for this time since their inception in Hyderabad in the 1930s.

This is an era in which one world story dies and another is born. 2012 became the symbolic date of transition.

2012 was also the year my eldest brother Glyn died. The accepted way to describe it would be to say he lost a four year battle with cancer. That was not quite my experience. Yes, he fought for life, to put his affairs in order before the cancer ate through his body one organ at a time. But in the end, in the final days he let go gracefully into the inevitable stream of death.

If I raked through the ashes of Glyn's death for clues about what of our era wants to die, it would be masculinity, or at least the caricature of masculinity we are asked to buy into. Strength at all cost, resolve, hard-work, powering through the stress, succeeding in a materialistic world. These were the things that killed him. The trappings of a millionaire lifestyle, topped off with the Standard American Diet. These and a little too much smoking and drinking in his younger days – habits formed to protect a vulnerability that felt out of place in a seemingly hostile world.

I could call this Toxic Masculinity, the self-destructive internalisation of the façade of masculinity given to us by a patriarchal culture. But that would be a disservice to my brother and his memory – perhaps to any man. It was more subtle than this, more nuanced. It was a drive to do well, to be of value, to succeed. It was a drive to provide for loved ones, to be special. At times it was generous to a fault. And at times the repressed anger that sat beneath it showed its shadow.

This sense of somehow being at odds with life, having to struggle and exert yourself at each turn, these were the things I saw Glyn let go of in his final days. Something tells me all this will need to die if we are to find a life at peace with ourselves and with the Earth that bears us. There are many things we hold dear that will end.

Freedom for one. It is a shallow illusion clung to all too tightly in the West. This reckless pursuit of individual freedom is a form of madness. We cannot survive on our own so why would we make this our highest political ideal? What would make us think that we can pursue our personal interest at the expense of others? It is a vain and fragile God hiding our deepest insecurities.

Comfort is another. The Easy Life is the enemy of the environment. It makes us soft and vain and pampered. It disconnects us from the natural world cosseting ourselves indoors like delicate blossoms.

And perhaps hardest of all, we are going to have to admit defeat. Admit that we tried the path of technology, growth, mastery over the

Earth and it has brought us to the brink of collapse. And despite our best intentions we have failed to change course and avoid disaster.

The only saving grace is that every end is also a beginning. I do not relish collapse. I love life too much for that. I do not wish disaster upon us because we deserve it. We do not. I am merely resigned to this being tougher than it need be. I have admitted defeat and now look forward to the new beginning.

Some say we are midwifing the new era while we hospice the old. One or other of these tasks is challenging enough. We have set ourselves the mission of doing both, simultaneously.

And if 2012 wasn't the moment, when is? The answer may well be that there will not be a moment. Transitions, transformations are just that – a slow fundamental change from one order to another. This will not be an event. It will be a process.

It is a coin-toss which will cause the collapse of the current global order: economic turbulence or environmental catastrophe. I have traced both forward as best I can. And as best as I can see, they seem to collide with each other around 2050, as my college hero suggests. At that time, run-away climate change kicks in, key resources (oil, the minerals in our phones) start to run out and a huge cyclical crash in the economy brings global markets to a meltdown.

Two years after his death my brother appeared to me in a dream. He brought two sentences, a single piece of advice for my life. And because he was my older brother, and I looked up to him, I have followed it: "Close down the ordinary. Leave space and energy for the extraordinary". Somehow I feel as though this has something to do with the way we will need to approach the transition of our age.

The Long Arc

The future is forgotten land
infinite potential,
longed-for memory
where sky meets earth in lingered kiss
and proud brown lioness beats out the path.
It confuses, with beauty, ecstatic pain
Entices, with excitement, adventure.

Language struggles to explain
why spirit craves nothing
soul seeks only acceptance, compassion, ease.

The long arc of horizon
bends towards night
tugging stars across sky.
It nudges me to step from this path to the next –
from destruction, the violence of separation
into unity.
It calls me to banish this lie,
to recall that the essence of love is surrender.
Patience, it purrs -
Hope is the last to die.
Kindness the easiest gift.

On this slow and constant curve
there is no point of no return.
Just gradual incline, eons long
promising light, dawn, forgetting.

I do not trust my judgement any more
don't know how to seize this moment
cannot tell how much I believe
can't rely on the lens I use to gauge the turning.

Still I crave a whole sea that shifts the world apace.
Still I know there is nothing to be done
but wait for the seventh wave
of the seventh generation
Then celebrate the fragile brilliance of each human soul
cast up on the beach
edges smoothed by time and tide.

Collective Poem[xxi]

Life Boats

"Don't spend all your energy protesting an obsolete system that's going to collapse anyways. Spend our energy rebuilding the sustainable systems our ancestors knew and loved and which we can bring back again. Build up those life boats because everyone's going to need those when the time comes and the crap hits the fan."

Lyla June Johnston, poet, songwriter and activist[xxii]

Return to the Source

There is something deeply significant about the transition we currently face. It is make or break for the human race – the first time in our existence that we could face extinction. It is an existential crisis.

How do you get through an existential crisis? All I know is how I navigated my own, in the dark nights of the soul that followed my brother's death. In amongst it all there was a point where I completely lost sight of who I was. Life and death seemed meaningless. The fragile construct I had created and called myself felt an irrelevance. Everything that had gone before seemed surreal, odd. It made no sense.

From this place the future is unclear. Because everything available now seems of no use, it is impossible to know how to proceed. There seem to be two possible responses to the near future (maybe more). Panic. Or Acceptance. No, acceptance isn't quite right. It's more a surrender. A giving up of human will. A giving over to the course of events.

I suspect, for this was my experience, that the difference in which path you choose, panic or surrender, depends on one thing: the degree to which you have a sense that there is something that lies at your very core. It is the part of you that has remained unchanged throughout life. What is your very essence, the true indomitable part, unique and powerful? In the depths of night it can be hard to grasp this but knowing there is something there and taking time to befriend it brings peace and new possibility. In time it becomes possible to identify this aspect of your essence. This is what will survive the transition. It is the part you were destined to reveal.

I have an inkling that it will be the same for humanity as a species. This is our existential crisis. The time for us to find ourselves again. We are lost in the shadow of our own worst excesses. We are lost in the undergrowth of human frailty, vanity, pain and humiliation. This is our moment of collective breakdown, and our opportunity to return to the source and find our essence.

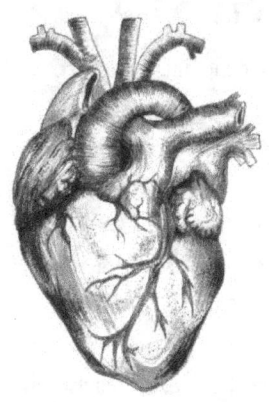

3. Breaking Point

What Comes on the Other Side of the Transformation?

This is a time of crisis and transition. The structure of things is sagging to breaking point. Do not be afraid to act alone. Push your principles and ideals beyond their normal limits. Have a noble purpose. There is a creative purpose at work in the breakdown.

If the situation does not nourish you, push it over and leave. Let the strong force gathering at the centre penetrate and move you. This is a very important time.

Do not act. Reimagine the situation. Retreating and joining with others brings profit and insight. Do not dwell in the past. See important people who can help you activate what is great in you. Though this is a difficult time, it carries the possibility of renovating your inner power and your connection to the way. Correct the way you use power.

[I Ching 28, Great Exceeding, transforming to 39, Difficulties]

A Difficult Time

So far, so good: a time of global transformation. I had known this was coming, sensed it in the early 1980s whilst sifting through the shelves of my college library in post-industrial Sunderland, finding the books that could track the system from its birth to its death. I had known, hoped, it would end in my lifetime.

But with the idealism of youth I had imagined that what came next was the golden era, utopia, a "higher" system based on equality, global unity, shared ownership. With the fall of the Berlin Wall that vision seemed to fall too. We saw all too clearly what past attempts at a more social world had created. As news trickled out of Kampuchea, China, the Soviet empire, we retrenched, regrouped, grasped for a more human, more humane model for the future. For me it would be thirty years before I found anything close to what I was looking for.

And then this Reading from the I Ching: "*A Time of Crisis*". What? After the demise of capitalism? No utopia then? We go through one almighty global collapse to be greeted not by Shangri La but by crisis, things sagging to breaking point?

This broke my heart. How could it be? How could my idealism be so misplaced, so off-the-mark? And how could we survive this – a double catastrophe? How would we be able to sustain our ideals, our dreams, our approach through a period where it seemed not to be working?

Sagging to Breaking Point

The best-selling environmental book of all time is 1972's The Limits to Growth. It was written by a group of politicians, industrialists and others calling themselves The Club of Rome. Translated into 30 languages, the premise of the book is simple – that the global economy cannot go on expanding forever, given that natural resources are finite.

A group of scientists from MIT in the US used early computer modelling to identify large scale economic trends and their impact on the world. Forty years later, researchers at University of Melbourne re-ran the models to see what came up. As one commentator put it:

> *The warnings that we received in 1972 ... are becoming increasingly more worrisome as reality seems to be following closely the curves that the ... scenario had generated.*[xxiii]

It's not a pretty picture. The conclusion was not simply that resources would run out but that this combined with environmental pollution would cause human populations to crash.

Their 1972 predictions for environment, economy and population (dotted lines in the graphs below) have proven remarkably accurate (solid lines) forty years on.

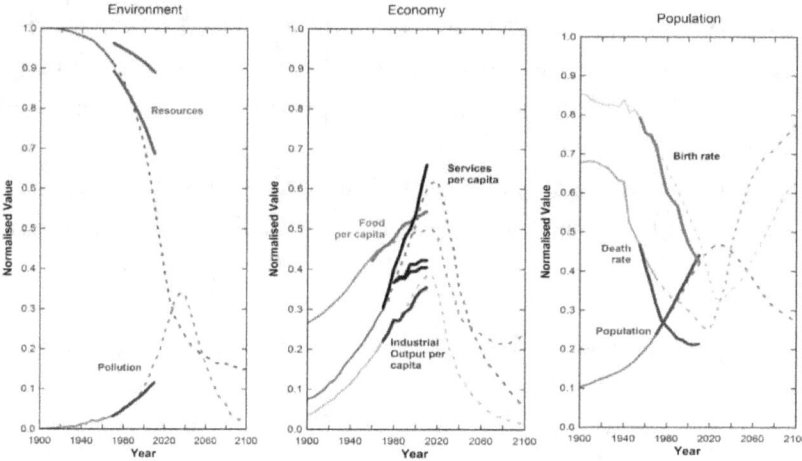

Figure 1. *LTG* BAU (Standard Run) scenario (dotted lines) compared with historical data from 1970 to 2010 (solid lines)—for demographic variables: population, crude birth rate, crude death rate; for economic output variables: industrial output per capita, food per capita, services per capita (upper curve: electricity p.c.; lower curves: literacy rates for adults, and youths [lowest data curve]); for environmental variables: global persistent pollution, fraction of non-renewable resources remaining (upper curve uses an upper limit of 150,000 EJ for ultimate energy resources; lower curve uses a lower limit of 60,000 EJ [Turner 2008]).

Despite all our best efforts and countless Climate Summits, we continue to head inexorably towards ecological disaster. The model predicts sudden and drastic collapse – sometime after 2020. This is when the graphs change direction – food production, industrial output and services all start to fall and as a result population tumbles. Rather matter-of-factly the 2012 report states:

> *Diminishing per capita supply of services and food causes a rise in the death rate from about 2020 (and a somewhat lower rise in the birth rate, due to reduced birth control options). The global population therefore falls, at about half a billion per decade, starting at about 2030.* [xxiv]

On these projections, we fall to a human population of around two billion instead of the current 7 billion (and growing). This process of collapse is predicted to be around the mid-point of this century. It can be delayed by about a decade via concerted action on climate change but this would actually make the eventual collapse even worse because of ongoing damage inflicted to other ecological systems in the meantime.

This is the tightrope we are walking. Trapped in a system that is devoid of morals and oblivious to its impact on the cosmic eco-system that bore it, every action has consequences we cannot imagine.

It is not easy to stare into the face of a global system falling apart. If the Club of Rome is to be believed it will not be pretty. We face hunger, disease, the collapse of industries that provide us with our consumer goods.

It is uncomfortable to think of a transformation followed by a crisis. If we have to go through a chaotic change we'd like to think there would be calm afterwards. It's natural to hope it will bring a resolution.

Here we're asked to consider something different. That the transformation will lead to another crisis. That one collapsing order will cause systems to sag to breaking point.

The longer we go on without addressing the environmental crisis the worse it gets. We can delay the crash but in doing so we make it faster and deeper when it comes.

Wake-Up Call

She was wearing a heart monitor for a month during the time of the Great American Eclipse. So she was acutely aware of the heartbeat of the Earth. She was always aware of the Earth's pulse within her own but it was heightened now – her own heart was telling her something.

The moment of the eclipse was beautiful and profound, yet eerie. The light darkened into a greenish dusk, the birds and insects fell silent, hushed. A strange peace fell upon the land as a lunar darkness crossed over the glaring solar light. For a few moments, we earthlings experienced a shift in our consciousness – a moment led by the moon, cooling the flames of the sun.

Her heart kept beating – or maybe it skipped a beat just then.

Then life went on. An astrologer told her that afterwards we might see some climate disruptions like earthquakes or floods. And with a fury they began. In Houston. In India and Nepal. In Bangladesh and Nigeria. Unprecedented floods and hurricanes. Monsoon rains like never before. Her heart skipped another beat and the tears began to fall. Then the fires came into view. Raging all over the western states with temperatures well into the 100s in places that should not get above 70. Fires destroying the ancient sequoias. Destroying whole watersheds of mountain wilderness and ravaging metropolitan communities in the southlands. No one was safe.

And still the denial was everywhere. It's a scam, they said, a propaganda tool. Others insisting that Nature is turning against us in response to a system so corrupted by power and wealth that it is blindly destroying the little wild left. Life out of balance. And still we pretend we are untouchable. Her heart skipped another beat. Then it began to race. It was hard to breathe. The smoke in the air was suffocating. Another crack in the ice reverberated along the Earth's songlines.

The trees stood still while the winds of change blew through their branches and the animals fled to the edges of their world. Where do we go now? The Great Turning. What kind of collective awakening is this? She became aware finally, that she was witnessing Mother Earth's demise. She hated to admit it. Had held for so long to the belief that humans would wake up – that even a small number of us would manage to turn the situation around. But no, she still knew there was goodness to be found in the hearts of many and she would hold to that in her own faltering heart. The tears fell again.

But the devastation and destruction occurring now was going to take lifetimes, eons to recover from. And in that time span an artificial world could take root upon the natural one, the cycle of slavery repeating itself, along with civil wars in every direction. It was inevitable now. Her heart raced. She breathed to calm it. This helped. Perhaps the flooded petro-chemical plants in the port of Houston would be a warning to the military industrial complex and CEOs would reorient themselves.

She took another breath. The end of nature. We are witnessing this. And it's coming faster and more furiously than anyone expected. Let's not pretend. We are not immune. And yet we can create the conditions for peace to prevail. For wisdom to arise. Compassionate actions are occurring everywhere. This is the spirit we must feed, she insisted. I will do this until my dying breath. With every beat of my heart. Life on Earth is a beautiful thing. We did see this coming. Let's not pretend otherwise. Now, let's cultivate kindness. Nurture our love. Let's open our hearts even wider and breathe to calm the storms. Suffering is everywhere. I vow to end it.

Cynthia Jurs, Founder, Earth Treasure Vase Initiative. xxv

Crisis and Transition

If you do not initiate the young men into the tribe, they will burn down the village just to feel the heat.

African Proverb

This is where we are. Humanity is a juvenile species, barely a few seconds old in geological time. Having discovered technology, science, the ability to conquer space, split the atom, we have become drunk on our own power. We are like an adolescent feeling the hormones of adulthood coursing through their veins for the first time.

The adolescent human race has gone on the rampage, flexing its muscles, pushing body and soul to breaking point to find the boundary. This is the first stage in the rite of passage to adulthood. But it is not the end of the story.

Many "traditional" societies (by which we mean societies that have retained the ability to live in harmony with the natural world) use a rite of passage to move from adolescence to adulthood. This is not merely a ceremonial marking of transition. More often than not it involves very real danger – having to face mortality, having to sacrifice something, risk something of yourself to calm the blood, to prove that you can take on the responsibilities of maturity. You have to face death to know how to live the life you are destined for.

If this ritual is not present our subconscious recreates it. We risk life and limb in foolish pursuits – drugs, alcohol, extreme sports. The archetypal process is so much a part of our make-up that our subconscious leads us on a path of risk and danger.

This is where we are. An adolescent drunk on possibility, frail of ego, unclear how to live a life of responsibility and due care. In cosmological time we are but a few moments since our first faltering baby steps out of Africa. And now, humanity as a species has pushed itself to the brink of death, wounded and trying desperately to prove its own worth.

This is why the crisis will play itself out, whether we like it or not. We have to face our own extinction as a species. It seems the only way we can grow up and take our place as grounded beings integrated into the web of life. Nothing less will cool the fever engulfing our collective psyche.

Creative Breakdown

In the Age of Decadence we await the fall. It is an archetypal period when some know what's coming and others are consumed by excess and avarice. Drama is ubiquitous, all consuming: political drama, sports, music, public entertainment. It is there to distract from the impending end, an almost conscious act on behalf of increasingly disparate rulers. But its real power lies in its subconscious hold on the majority who have intuited the absurdity of the times and integrated that absurdity into their lives.

It is no coincidence that this lets loose a fountain of diverse creative juices. Strange times lead to strange deeds. There seems no point in careful, dedicated action. Only flamboyance, entrepreneurism, expression feel right.

Yet the breakdown itself will be the most creative act. All the pieces will fall to the ground to be reassembled in whatever way we see fit. Transformation is not to be feared, although that is often the first response. It is easier to look back than move forward. Better the devil you know… But transformation always leads to somewhere with new potential. Even death is a liberation for those left behind.

After collapse comes a period of reorganisation and eventual regeneration. This cannot happen without collapse. Archaeologists have noticed patterns that sometimes occur[xxvi]. One is a levelling off. Wealth is redistributed. Taxes tend to disintegrate as the social fabric frays. The edifices built on tax revenues fall and ordinary people have more income (at least those who survive). Writings from ancient Egypt record a period when this happened:

> *Lo, the nobles lament, the poor rejoice… He who was a great man now performs his own errands. Precious stones adorn the necks of maidservants, and men who used to wear fine linen are beaten.*[xxvii]

Key skills, practical skills needed to rebuild become sought-after and the pay of ordinary folk increases. So the new is built from the ruins of the old. The breakdown becomes a breakthrough. Unless things decay they cannot be composted. This is the essence of rebirth, new life and progress.

To what Extent will the Transition be Apocalyptical?

This is a time of transition. Be very small. Keep your power hidden by carefully adapting to each thing that crosses your path. Do not under any circumstances seek to impose your will. This will bring you success, profit and insight.

Confine yourself to small things. By being exceedingly small and careful, the great way will open. Concentrate on the details.

You are over-reaching yourself and are in real danger. If you go on like this you may be killed. The way is closed. Abandon this way of proceeding.

Take a look at what has happened in the recent past and let it be a warning to you. Do not always repeat the same mistake.

This is the primal power to nourish and give things form – the Earth, the Moon, the mother. This can open a whole new cycle of time. Make sure you keep your sense of inner purpose. The way is open to you through calm, quiet acceptance. Let your power to realize things be so generous that it can carry everything that approaches. Cherish each thing and let it grow.

[I Ching 62, Small Exceeding; transforming to 2, Field]

Very Real Danger

In the spring of 2019, or so it seemed, all of a sudden everyone started talking about collapse. Or the possibility of human extinction. Or runaway climate emergency.

Everything seemed to happen at once. The UN gave us 12 years to stop global warming. The antics of the latest US President seemed to suggest the world's hegemonic power was in a state of disarray, flailing around franticly in an attempt to regain lost greatness.

Greta Thunberg took the world by storm. An unlikely hero of the hour – a fifteen year old autistic schoolgirl who refused to play by the rules of established protest. Greta said what everyone was thinking and was too polite to say out loud. She told a packed room of world leaders at 2018's UN Climate Change Conference:

> *You only talk about moving forward with the same bad ideas that got us into this mess. Even when the only sensible thing to do is to pull the emergency break.*

After berating them for being unable to recognise and speak the truth, she continued:

> *We are about to sacrifice our civilisation for the opportunity of a very small number of people to continue to make enormous amounts of money. We are about to sacrifice the biosphere so that rich people in countries like mine can live in luxury. but it is the sufferings of the many which pay for the luxuries of the few...*

> *You say that you love your children above everything else. And yet you are stealing their future. Until you start focussing on what needs to be done rather than what's politically possible, there's no hope.*

> *And if solutions within the system are so impossible to find then maybe we should change the system itself?*

> *We have not come here to beg world leaders to care. You've run out of excuses and we're running out of time. We've come here to let you know that change is coming whether you like it or not. Real power belongs to the people.*[xxviii]

In Greta's wake, Extinction Rebellion exploded onto the scene. It was the movement I'd been waiting for – forensically focussed on the issue of the moment while keeping a firm eye on the long term transformation of human civilisation. It was more than a climate protest group. It was the prefiguration of a new world run on principles of non-violence, anti-oppression and care for all life.

Like many in the UK I have jumped feet first into the Extinction Rebellion movement. It has captured something in the zeitgeist, bringing together people across cultures and generations in a movement for fundamental global change. It's not just about climate change. It's about a revolution of love, deep ecology and radical transformation.

As time went on, many in the movement began to wonder if we'd make it. Was it all too little too late? Figures began to circulate – only a billion would survive, maybe half a billion. And meanwhile species were going extinct at unprecedented rates. Many of us were overcome with grief, darkness, foreboding.

At the same time, voices like Jem Bendell[xxix] were calling us to come to terms with the fact that social collapse was inevitable. We had to face up to the fact. Anything else was just denial.

I had first experienced the notion of complete civilisational collapse in 2015 when I attended a seminar by the US climate scientist Guy McPherson. Guy had become fixated on the multiple feedback loops that arise once climate change starts to take hold. He became convinced that they would unleash such force that global temperatures would rise much further than expected, causing much of the world to become uninhabitable. This led him to the term Near Term Human Extinction. We were all, ALL, going to die.

I remember sitting in a community centre in the ancient English city of York, forcing myself to take this seriously, to let it sink into my bones. My overriding emotion was one of sadness. It might have been sadness for the loss of human life, or for the destruction that would be caused. The untold misery and suffering for billions of people I didn't even know.

But actually, it was sadness for something slightly different. It was the sense that we had come so close to realising our greatness and then fallen at the last hurdle. So close, only to trip ourselves on the home stretch. I couldn't quite accept that it might end this way. Over the intervening four years I would have no choice but to come to terms with this possibility.

Be Very Small

Keep your power hidden. Do not impose your will. Confine yourself to small things. These are the mantras of a revolution without arms.

It is not how you would normally conceive a revolution. In my studies of political science, power wins out and the powerful never give up privilege without a struggle.

So much might be true but this Reading asks us to imagine another way, to build a new form of revolution where we reinvent the entire world without imposing our will. If we are to avoid the Global Transformation slipping into an apocalyptical power struggle, we are asked to find a way forward where we are small, act small, avoid overstretching ourselves. We will need to let go of all anger, bitterness, resentment, and struggle for power.

This is a Herculean task – of restraint, inclusion, integration. We must build on yielding, side-step aggression, concentrate on small things from which the future grows. Tend seeds literal and metaphorical. Nurture children of the future.

Across the world we are discovering and rediscovering methodologies to support this process of presencing. Many involve bringing in more intuition to allow us to sense into the unknown. Socio-drama, Social Presencing Theatre, Systemic Constellations all use our innate capacity to draw information from The Field, or as Jung called it The Collective Unconscious.

It seems there is an iterative exchange between personal and global change. This to-ing and fro-ing creates a momentum which builds to becomes a wave. As Charles Eisenstein suggests[xxx], we do not make a movement. It makes us. If the revolution leaves us unchanged it has merely been a coup. We have fooled ourselves into accepting a new boss – the same as the old boss. Revolution without personal transformation is a mirage.

Rhon Fabian, who wrote the passage about sitting by the river, is editor of Kosoms Journal and a media educator. In collaboration with Dr Jennifer Horner, she has researched the Global Transformation Movement, a convergence of conscious efforts that is arising to shape and be shaped by our fast-changing world. She identifies five insights about this movement:

1. The Global Transformation Movement is self-organising.
2. It manifests as a values-driven 'movement of movements'.
3. The Movement uses alternative forms of learning.
4. It emphasises improvisation.
5. Global Transformation embraces a spiritual approach to change.[xxxi]

This is exactly what I'd found in Extinction Rebellion and before that in Occupy. I'd observed it from afar in the Arab Spring and movements like Black Lives Matter. The point being, everywhere we seem to be entering into an era of Global Presencing. To a greater or lesser extent the whole of humanity stepping into the process of global change without knowing how it can be done or where it might end.

Tried and tested solutions no longer work. The desperate or powerful apply them with ever greater feverishness. The rest stand and watch bewildered or outraged. It is time to stop. It is time to allow the future to emerge. To find enough stillness to hear its whisper. We will not create the future. It will create us.

Hasta La Revolution

Che Guevara, that icon of sixties revolutionary chic rode into Havana on a tank on my birth date – several years before I was born. It was the day a regime famed for its corruption, repression and decadence fell to the will of a rag-tag army of idealists.

Unable to see himself as anything other than a revolutionary Che moved on to the next struggle, leaving Fidel Castro to become the darling of the world's socialist dreamers. After the revolution, faced with crippling sanctions, Cuba developed strong ties with the Soviet Union, entering into reciprocal trade agreements.

One unintended consequence of the fall of the Berlin Wall was the collapse of these trade relationships – not only in Cuba but across the entire "socialist bloc". As the Soviet Union crumbled, these arrangements became less sustainable and Cuba lost a cheap supply of oil and essential food imports which supplemented what was grown domestically.

Already cut off from wider trade by a punishing US blockade, Cuba now lost its principal trade partner. As a result Cubans on average lost access to one third of their food calories. Not only this, faced with a lack of oil, the government decided to curtail production of fertilizers and the use of tractors.

Faced with a crisis in food production, this small Caribbean Island had to completely overhaul its approach to food production. The result is a system of de facto organic production which uses all available spaces in towns and cities to grow food. This includes more than 8,000 "parcelas" or small garden lots in Havana, rooftop livestock farms (for chickens, Guinea pigs and rabbits) and the use of permaculture techniques[xxxii].

As systems sag to breaking point, as global capitalism collapses into ruins, our salvation lies in small things, careful things, things that do not overstretch us or repeat the mistakes of the past.

Another World

Another world does not exist
There is only this –
Past, present, future
not always in that order,
inner, outer, unity.

Another world does not exist
There is only this –
unhealthy social constructs
our sense of self-importance
our sense of self as separate beings
giving way
to collective being,
giving way
to the wild intuitive voice within.

Another world does not exist.
There is only peace of mind
understanding that thought creates feeling
feeling creates experience
experience creates understanding of each other.

Another world looks people in the eye
invoking faith in humanity
asking us to be all we can be.
I long for a world.

Another world does not exist
There is only
this joy and beauty
that rushes toward me
and through me
in this and any world.

Collective Poem

I Hear Her Breathing

If we look at this conflict as a straightforward eye-ball to eye-ball confrontation between 'Empire' and those of us who are resisting it, it might seem that we are losing. But there is another way of looking at it. We, all of us gathered here, have, each in our own way, laid siege to 'Empire.' We may not have stopped it in its tracks – yet – but we have stripped it down. We have made it drop its mask. We have forced it into the open. It now stands before us on the world's stage in all its brutish, iniquitous nakedness.

Empire may well go to war, but it's out in the open now – too ugly to behold its own reflection. Too ugly even to rally its own people.

Before September 11th 2001, America had a secret history. Secret especially from its own people. But now America's secrets are history, and its history is public knowledge. It's street talk.

What can we do? We can hone our memory, we can learn from our history. We can continue to build public opinion until it becomes a deafening roar. We can re-invent civil disobedience in a million different ways. In other words, we can come up with a million ways of becoming a collective pain in the ass.

Our strategy should be not only to confront empire, but to lay siege to it. To deprive it of oxygen. To shame it. To mock it. With our art, our music, our literature, our stubbornness, our joy, our brilliance, our sheer relentlessness – and our ability to tell our own stories. Stories that are different from the ones we're being brainwashed to believe.

The corporate revolution will collapse if we refuse to buy what they are selling – their ideas, their version of history, their wars, their weapons, their notion of inevitability. Remember this: We be many and they be few. They need us more than we need them.

Another world is not only possible, she is on her way. On a quiet day, I can hear her breathing.

Arundhati Roy, author and social activist[xxxiii]

4. A Favourable Time

How will the Planet Fare Over the Coming Century?

A time to welcome what comes to you. Acting through the woman and the yin brings invigorating strength. Do not try to enforce your will. This is a time of meetings, brief, intense encounters that involve universal forces. Do not try to control them directly but realise what happens to you reflects the union of these powers.

Great things are moving in these events. The spirit spreads throughout the world. You are coupled with a creative force. It brings unexpected encounters, lucky coincidences and enjoyable happenings. When heaven and earth meet, all the beings join in a brief radiant display. The time of welcoming and coupling is truly great.

Something significant is approaching. This is the point of first contact, the arrival of the new. This particularly describes the approach of something great and powerful to something smaller. Look after things with care and sympathy. Keep your expectations modest. The contact can open a whole new time. It brings fundamental success, profit and insight. This is a particularly favourable time for what is growing, so do not rush to complete things. This will not be an early harvest. It is the return of the great.

[I Ching 44, Coupling; transforming to 19, Nearing]

A Time to Welcome

And so, after collapse and crisis, the deepest winter storm, there comes light, rebirth. A time when Universal forces are at play.

As we move into the 22nd Century, a radiant display sweeps the face of the world. Springtime for a New Earth. The opening of a whole new time. Utopia postponed – provided we maintain our focus on small things, do not get above ourselves, hold to our principles, avoid a retreat into past ways.

What a relief this was to read.

Universal Forces

The Earth has a say in her own becoming[xxxiv]. She is not an inert mass but a thriving, living entity. Her spirit is the spirit of Gaia that spurs all things to life. Her soul, the soul of Hestia, the hearth around which comfort gathers and community learns to shape its destiny. To forget this is the ultimate act of human arrogance – anthropocentrism personified.

The subtle voice of the Earth plays out in energy, intuition, omens and signs. It does not shout to be heard, for it knows sometimes it will not be. It relies on other beings to pay attention, to inhabit a state of mind that interprets, notices, responds without thought. A state of being that is prepared to follow, that feels safe enough to move within a flow without needing to fight against it.

Do you feel safe enough to abandon the illusion of free will? Freedom is a tin-pot dictator stuck together from cast-off pieces of ego, vanity and self-delusion. There is no freedom, only interdependence. For those wise enough to notice, this is the subtle art of moving in and with the flow of time.

This flow is moving now, gathering momentum. It is moving through us, tugging at our primordial self. Universal forces are moving through us, igniting a forgotten code in our DNA.

We will not save the world without relearning something of her ways. Gaia is alive and ready to teach. In the same way the human body only lives thanks to the balance of billions of bacteria in our gut, so the world is a living body kept healthy by the balance of life forces within it.

There are laws that govern the health of Gaia. Natural Laws. Disregard them and balance is lost. All life becomes in peril until a dynamic shifting equilibrium is restored. This is the Law of Dynamic Equilibrium, of Predictor and Prey. Balance is maintained by the interplay between the lives that feed off and into each other.

Things move in waves, cycles of life and death. Impermanence. This is the Law of Rebirth. Then there is the Law of Interbeing. Nothing is itself without its relationships to everything else. Mutual dependence. I breathe in what trees breathe out. Microbes eat what I excrete. There is no waste. Just food for something else. These are the laws we must reintegrate into our way of being. These are the laws the longest living civilisations on the planet, those we call indigenous, have lived by.

To restore balance will require some healing. The impact of rampant human over-activity has been to shift the composition of the air, to deplete the composition of the soil and pollute the life-giving water.

The first can be restored by plants, especially trees. So can the second and even the third. We will need an Age of Plants to heal the excesses of the Age of People. This will mean not just planting trees but living more like them. Sit with a tree and you come to realise you need time to know the tree, to understand it. Moments matter less than seasons. A tree breathes in and out with the changing seasons – in with winter, out into the green of summer. Things are slower, take longer, are kinder and gentler. More forgiving.

We will not save the world without becoming more like a tree or the land, a lake or a landscape.

A Radiant Display

It is not hard to imagine a world beyond the frantic materialism of the current order. It is imminent in the cracks in the paving stones of commodification. It is in the caring for a dying relative, the loan of a cup of flour to a neighbour. It is the feeling of satisfaction in helping a stranger find their way in the city, time spent with friends breaking bread. It is kith and kin, gifts given expecting nothing in return.

These things are the natural course of human encounter. They are present in any community, wherever it exists, whatever its history. They reveal the caring, loving side of human nature that nourishes both giver and receiver. It is not hard to follow your heart, to be moved by generosity or simple kindness.

Nor is it hard to imagine a different relationship to the world. This too is written into our DNA. Moments spent in reverence of the stars on a clear night. Silent stillness inspired by the presence of a deer glimpsed in the forest. Tender care given to house plants arranged on the kitchen window sill.

These are the moments that by-pass the gradual encroachment of the market. These are the moments when the brighter side of human nature rises to the surface.

And we will be surprised by the speed at which we can help Mother Earth to heal herself. Some things might take eons. The half-life of Chernobyl, Fukushima and a pantheon of decommissioned atomic facilities, the gradual decay of depleted uranium munitions will live on in the deformed DNA of several generations to come.

Other wounds will be quicker to heal. Any amount of vegetation will self-seed the cover that's needed to capture water in the desert. Trees will take decades but will provide shade, their roots binding the soil, their leaves capturing the rain. Within years, life will regenerate itself. All we need do is a bit of planting here, pruning there, irrigation where needed. If you've ever started a garden from nothing or been to a permaculture farm you'll know how possible this is.

All we need do is to dedicate ourselves to sieving the plastic from the oceans, the electronic waste from the soil, the particulates from the air. And planting. Planting stuff everywhere. When in doubt, plant trees.

Wherever possible grow food. The spirit of the Earth will flow through the soil once we let it. The breath of the air will flow freely. The energy of water that cleans everything and nourishes all life, needs only to be set free and left untethered. The four elements have all they need to set Gaia on a course to a vibrancy and abundance we have not seen in years. Nature is her own healer. Nature is her own gardener. Because we are Nature.

And we have learnt already how to heal the Earth. While industrial agriculture has been gradually depleting the soil and drowning rivers in chemicals, others have been developing approaches to restore entire landscape, roll back the deserts and grow food in abundance.

But note, this will not be an early harvest. It will take time and patience to regenerate. It requires an attitude of being something small approached by something bigger – the greater knowledge and wisdom of Nature herself.

A Time for What's Growing

A force of Nature is spreading across the face of the Earth. Starting at the margins where it hibernated through the long cold Age of Winter, it has passed the fragile stage of early growth and is starting to flex its muscles. Soon it will understand it is strong enough to keep going, until one day it is the essence of a new world, growing in the ruins of an old.

Over recent years I have become aware of two movements which could help to trigger the type of renewal of the global eco-system envisaged in this Reading. The first is permaculture, the second Regenerative Landscape Management. Both seek to renew the health of soil and to increase diversity of produce through the use of organic inputs and the avoidance of chemicals during the growing process.

John Dennis Liu has made massive strides in helping to regenerate landscapes in a wide range of situations where human activity has degraded them. This includes the Loess Plateau in China, areas of Ethiopia and more recently in the Middle East. His work is inspirational in its long term impact. It shows that careful management of water, soil and vegetation can help restore land that had been decertified or otherwise eroded by over-use.

The Loess Plateau project has been described as "among the largest and most successful erosion control programs in the world" and lasted for over a decade. It successfully raised vegetation cover in the area from 17% back up to 40%. This in turn helped reduce erosion and flow of soil into the Yellow River by a massive 110 million tons. Improvements in farming helped raise living standards across a large area, bringing around 2.5 million people out of poverty. [xxxv]

Permaculture takes this kind of natural regeneration process and places it within a framework of ethics and principles for sustainable living. Its three core principles are care for people, care for earth and equitable sharing of resources. A key tenet is to observe and interact before intervening in the eco-system. Usually this means observing an entire annual cycle through the seasons. This way we learn what the landscape needs; how plants, animals and water interact. We observe the effects of sun, shade and wind. We adopt a more humble approach. We learn from Nature, then act in ways that enhance her own power, flow and growth.

Other systems sharing a similar ethos are emerging, including agroforestry. This combines trees and food crops in a symbiotic process, thus increasing yields of both. Agroforestry has taken root in areas of Brazil where forests are being protected alongside agriculture.

All these systems seek to understand how nature works, to mimic it, learn from it and use its power to produce abundance. They work with nature and its flow rather than seeking to stamp an artificial pattern upon it.

Ernst Gotsch, the founder of the Brazilian Agroforestry movement says:

> *Humans could reconcile themselves with the planet, finding a way to be useful and welcomed in the system, but we don't realise that and we can't see because we have disconnected ourselves from life on the planet, thinking that we are the intelligent ones. We can't see that we are just part of an intelligent system.*[xxxvi]

Becoming Indigenous

There is something about our moment on the arc of time that calls us to reconnect to our sense of oneness with the wonder of existence. It calls us to rediscover this felt-sense that indigenous peoples have kept alive for all of humanity, despite our best efforts to wipe them off the face of the Earth.

It serves no-one to fetishize or appropriate the traditions of another's heritage. This is not about buying crystals, dream-catchers, sweat lodge experiences. It is about rediscovering a deeper connection to that part of the human soul that craves connection to Mother Earth, the star-encrusted heavens, the consciousness behind the eye of an animal companion.

It is about 'becoming indigenous', having the time to listen to the cries, and signs and warnings of the world around. It is about spending time in deep contemplation and allowing the future to merge into our consciousness. It is about shifting the locus from action to allowance.

For those still in connection with their heritage and their ancient wisdom teachings, there is a thread to follow – however frail this may have been worn by the ravages of colonialism and globalisation.

For others of us, our lineage has been all but severed. Uprooted from the land, driven into cities, wrenched from the ancients who kept our accumulated knowledge, we are rootless, placeless. We may be victors in the scramble for material accumulation but this comes at a cost to our souls.

It is hard to hear the future above the constant chatter of smartphones, Facebook feeds, twitter storms, 24hour news – fake or otherwise. It's hard to hear the future above our own dissatisfaction with current events: shouting at the news means we have scarce little bandwidth for a distant whisper. Ego is noisy when left to its own devices.

There is one sure way. The pull of the land is strong. It sucks us from the city at the weekend. It calls throughout the year until we cannot resist embracing it during vacations. We invite the land into our worlds, in easily manageable chunks – window boxes, pets, house plants. We venture out in equally un-disruptive spells – park runs, beach walks, weekends in the garden.

There is peace in the outdoors. Health, healing, rejuvenation. Is it possible the land can teach us the secret of the future? Native American elder Kahontakwas Diane Longboat believes so:

> *We're told that Mother Earth is indigenizing all of us. That we are in a time and we are in a place where everything that we need to know about the future is going to come from the land. The land is going to tell us how to live, how to correct our behaviour, how to conserve and how to be good citizens in concert with Natural Law.*

> *The land is going to be reminding us of the rules of life because we as human beings have fallen out of balance with that. The land is going to shift our governance structures. It's going to shift our economy and it's going to shift the way we teach, the way we pursue our health, the way that we achieve mental health and wellbeing. The land is going to shift everything. The land is going to indigenize us.*[xxxvii]

What might the land teach us if we were to listen to her for a moment? How to be at peace. How to wonder at the awe of a landscape. How to walk lightly leaving scarcely a trace of our passing foot. How to feed ourselves and the soil in the process. Limitless patience and forgiveness. To weather a storm and welcome the freshness that follows. To find food, water, shelter, medicine. To hold grief and release it into the night. All these things and more.

From here we can write the stories again, in song, in paint, in dance. Stories of homage to the wider cosmos. Stories of witness to our place in the natural order. Stories that warn of getting above and beyond ourselves. As we dance them back into our bodies and into the Earth, we reignite a creative impulse that has been lost to all but a few "artists".

Creativity is our natural state. It arises in us all when we lean into the rhythm of life. It is what makes us human, what opens our heart, what feeds our eye. Without it life is brutal and shallow, taking place in a hostile universe. We reclaim our creative essence, hand in hand with the muses and the genius that guide our hand and feet and lips.

For this spirit to spread across the face of the world brings a return to the natural order of Heaven and Earth.

Listening to the Land

I can offer an anecdote, from a time I was visiting the retirement estate of John Ruskin, the Victorian art critic, visionary and nature advocate. It's a stunning estate on the hillside overlooking Coniston Water in England's Lake District.

There is a calmness in the air, a deep green in the timeless hills. Our guide, a crusty friend named Sally, dying of cancer and resembling Ruskin more the older she gets, walks us around the meadow on the lakeside. "Walk in silence. Notice with each step. Listen to the Land, what she wants, what she has to offer." As I turn back at the far end of the meadow, the reply comes clear as a bell: "Accomplish more by doing less." This is the lesson of the land.

Upon returning home I was reminded of a chapter in the Tao Te Ching written by the ancient Chinese philosopher Lao Tzu two and a half millennia ago:

> *Those who think to win the world*
> *By doing something to it,*
> *I see them come to grief.*
> *For the world is a sacred object.*
> *Nothing is to be done to it.*
> *To do anything to it is to damage it.*
> *To seize it is to lose it.*[xxxviii]

Something happens when you enter into relationship with a piece of land. It sets up roots in a part of you that you haven't used before. From there it grows slowly, unnoticed until you find you have fallen in love.

Time moves at a different pace. Hours pass in a slow blur. With each turn of spade, each seed planted, life's cares fade. This is a space measured in seasons, not seconds. It takes three seasons for carrots to grow, or kale. You will need to plant fruit bushes several years before they bear fruit. Decades for apples or pears. This is a commitment. It is not an early harvest.

Return to the Great

Hubris is a jealous beast. It puffs up the human chest, intoxicates the brain, flexes muscle we never knew we had. There is a rush of blood that makes one feel invincible. The things is, it encourages us to overreach. It turns a gift, a strength, into its shadow. It's the ultimate shadow worker. The brightest sun casts the deepest shade.

Perhaps this is why it plays such a prominent role in tragedy. It is so easy to overstep the line of authenticity and become the opposite of who we are, what we have to offer.

So it has become for the human species. Intoxicated, we place ourselves above all else, above the Laws of Nature, beyond the Arc of the Universe. Drunk on pride we claim dominion over Nature, forgetting our innate love for her.

Such a small trick of the mind to believe that we can conquer nature, rise above it, shape it in every way to meet our every base desire.

And if it is such a small step off the path, then it is an equally small step back on again. Not such a monumental task to return to our authentic purpose, to find the great in our species for the future. Such a small step from greatness to grandeur, from humility to hubris. And such a small step back again.

The Spirit Spreads

The future sings from the depths of our hearts, pleading with us to listen to our deepest yearnings, to recognise in them a past and future Utopia. It shakes its head when we dismiss our own most firmly held beliefs, calling them childish or idealistic.

"Look!" it says. "I'm here. Feel this. It sings throughout your whole being. How can it possibly be wrong."

Imagine the buzz. A world finding its feet, yawning itself awake. As the grip of materialism loosens we turn towards something else. There is plenty to do. There are wounds to heal: the inherited trauma of genocide, child sexual abuse, lifetimes of micro-aggressions.

There are systems to reinvent: production, learning, sharing, building. And without profit to motivate action, what fills the void?

The answer is spirit. The spirit spreads to fill the cracks where the old system crumbles, the spirit of human warmth, of nature, the spirit of generosity and love. The spirit of cooperation. How do we pull together to rebuild? It's always the way. A challenge, the bigger the better, brings out the best in folk. Ego disappears, cooperation is no longer a value, but a necessity. Creativity unleashed stirs the heart, steadies the legs, recharges energy.

There is a human world to rebuild, a natural world to repair, a spiritual world to regain. Let the spirit free. It will guide you to the More Beautiful World your heart longs for.

So what are the wildest winds that blow through the forest of our dreams, rattling leaves, moaning through the branches of ancient oaks?

Our bodies long for a connection to the Earth, to lie in her firm, safe embrace. Our eyes long to see the landscape renew itself as the light of dawn sweeps across its back. Our ears crave the laughter of children, the ecstatic vibration of dance and song. Our hearts seek only to love and be loved. To give selflessly to those around us and receive the same warm embrace.

This is the dream of the coming age. A possible world built on the call of our bodily senses.

We all carry a seed of the More Beautiful World. None has it all. Each has a contribution. It sits deep inside, is fed by our own unique gifts. In combination they are combustible. It takes a village to raise a child. It takes a commune of gifts to birth the future.

Reach for your childish belief, your deepest longings, flimsiest ideals. Touch your deepest wound. The place that feels raw reminds you of the love you long to give to the world.

Cosmic Saga

Your life's work is an intergenerational project – that is because we are produced by the manifold, by the collective, so that to squeeze the significance of one's life into the container of its biological duration is to lose sight of the ways death is generative and prolific – and even useful for continuity. It is to centre the human in the very middle of a cosmic saga, all the while forgetting that the human is ecstatically mediated by, and dependent upon, and threaded through with, the nonhuman. It is to relinquish our accountability to our ancestors, who often need healing and continue to produce effects.

Our bodies are long bodies, wide bodies, spread out, queering space and time; your failure, your confusion, might well be the nourished soil that coaxes out new possibilities from the earth. Our work is long, unusual and always yet to be fully disclosed. The anorexic confines of traditional activisms cannot understand this or appreciate why many now feel invited to lean on the fences of conventional, intelligible action – even if it means being branded mad.

Your life's work is an intergenerational project, an ancestral conspiracy, a continuous meeting of bodies, a queering of temporality. Your life is not yours to resolve, yours to complete, or yours to contain. You will not finally be decolonized; you will not finally be enlightened; you will not finally be 'good' – no matter how conscientious, aware, 'woke' or alive you are. It is because your life is necessarily the life of the many – blessed with shadows, inner workings, sedimentation, ruptures, departures, arrivals, and frayed edges. Be thankful for the threadbare places of your life, for it gives the many who are yet to come something to stitch theirs with.

Adebayo C. Akomolafe[xxxix]

Love of the Land

Land calls
in dreams and visions, vistas, views and turned corners
I am all you need:
remedy for bruised bones and broken hearts
patience to mull every moment's care
space to let them fall silent under foot
to become loam for next season's growth.

Nature beckons
from tree and field, river, hill and sudden outcrop
Come find all you need:
food for heart and soul, belly, brain and furrowed brow
reason to give and share, lust and care
purpose to come together and remember
yourself – the part of you in every other
your essence in each bud and blade, pebble, thorn and
bloodied corpse.

Water waits
through fire and ice, death, dawn, moon and empire's
passing
pausing for storm to cull the faint, proud and luckless
before blowing itself out in dawn's hazy come-down.
Time is at my beck and call
medicine for misfortune, greed and grief
time is our mutual friend
happy we met
certain we were destined to find a place to raise generations
free to roam unfettered through path, peak and untold
fortune.

Abundance oozes from hedge, garden plot and orchard tree
pours from the hill and field
asking nothing in return save a passing conversation

a little love and attention
a foot dancing lightly on the clod.

To be held amid this plenty
is to feel the certainty of life and love
to touch a vein of wealth so deep
it dissolves all uncertainty.
There is only now.
There is only everything you ever need
here, always, at your gift
in exchange for grace.

5. Brighten Your Innate Pattern

What is the Nature of the Society that Replaces Capitalism?

Hide your intelligence and awareness to protect yourself. Enter what is beneath you. There is a real possibility of injury here. Accept drudgery, hard work where you see yourself at a disadvantage. This drudgery and difficulty will bring you profit and insight in the end.

Hide yourself in common labour. Deliverance is already being prepared so accept what confronts you. You are being excluded from the centre of things. Brighten your innate pattern. Use the enveloping obscurity to clarify your worthy ideas. Knowing how to distinguish what is right in a dark time will make you an inspiration to others.

[I Ching 36. Hiding Brightness]

Innate Pattern

These are tender truths that build a more beautiful world. The quiet, persistent sensations that tell us what's true and right. The soft reassuring voice that reminds us that what seems impossible has already occurred somewhere along the Arc of Time.

When asked to connect to what burns in our hearts, there is no disagreement amongst us. We reach instinctively for the most delicate corners of our soul. There are no divisions here. Doctrine, ideology, theoretical constructs melt into ether. Documenting the failings of the current order or arguing over which of the myriad solutions will contribute most to change, lose meaning. In our hearts we reach instead for the eternal truth of a life in balance, halfway between Heaven and Earth.

Once we lift ourselves into the heart-space of the yearning future we come home to the most fundamental and regenerative aspects of the human soul.

First there is a longing for peace. This is more than the absence of war. It is an active process of weaving a culture of non-violence, extreme inclusion, the active honouring, valuing and nurturing of diversity. It is in peace that our soul relaxes, letting go of the grief that chokes us. Letting go of the pain that twists and grinds our bones when we live in a world full of destruction, hatred and violence.

This gives rise to the tug of community. The yearning to be in intimate relationship with people who matter to us, who share an endeavour, who contribute to each other's growth and wellbeing. This is the urge to be seen and valued and at the same time to be of service. We want deeply to contribute to a place that feels good, that encourages, nurtures, creates: flaws and all. It is in inclusion of our imperfections that we find an end to resistance, conflict and aggression.

This in turn reveals a place of justice. From our first faltering steps we carry with us throughout life an antenna that senses relationships not on equal terms, any interaction that exerts undue power over us, or those close to us. We know what is right. It feels uneasy when we see another abused or mistreated. We wince at the overly stern word, the punitive fist, the derisory laugh. We grieve in the face of institutionalised violence and oppression, and for those who are traumatised enough to inflict it.

This is our innate pattern. The true, constant essence of human nature that lies beneath frail ego, insecurities and fear. Harmony, Connection, Justice. Human life is impossible without these and immeasurably enhanced the more of them we give and receive.

There is a dark side to human nature. We see this only too well in this, the era of decadence, selfishness and deceit. We are capable of inhuman acts of torture, oppression and hatred. But if we learn anything from the past it is that circumstances shape human actions again and again. It is the context around us that brings out the best or the basest instincts within us.

At heart we are lovers and dreamers. Our bones crave closeness, our muscles ache for creative release. We are called to use our bodies to build, shape, paint, sculpt. Our eyes insist we make our surroundings pleasant, full of beauty, balance, colour and shade. There is something deep within us that is tuned to bringing life, abundance, aesthetic – not just the utilitarian but the beautiful, the extra element that creates song and music. We paint before we can write, dance before we can walk, hum before we can talk. We are brighter than we know.

A Day in the Life

Spring has come late this year. It seemed for a while like it might not come at all. The fields were drowned all winter long, from rain upon rain that followed the thaw of snow. Farmers spoke with furrowed brows that the grass was not growing and the winter feed was nearly exhausted. Now everyone is amazed: only three days of sunshine have propelled spring in all her glory to burst forth from hedge and tree, soil and field.

Another cold snap does nothing to deter the growth and a blazing hot week has us all out in the Walled Garden. In twos and fours we dig holes a foot apart and carefully transfer the seedlings grown in the greenhouse over winter months. An afternoon's work sets out enough kale, cabbage and peas to last the year. Elsewhere some are picking purple broccoli, the earliest yield to fill the Hunger Gap.

Under the shade of apple blossom three sets of children paddle in the balmy heat, overseen by someone's parents. Out of sight a field is ploughed for barley, friends sit beside the lake whiling away the time, families share Sunday dinners.

It has not always been like this. There have been times of anger and dispute when livelihoods clash with high ticket maintenance costs, or grudges fester. But for now things run smooth; harmonious. The rotas are filled without the need of a heavy hand. The animals are tended, food is planted, spaces are cleaned. And time is given to community.

Yesterday was more restful. A day of exchanging songs from near and far: Te Aroha: Peace to You; Heno, Ben Blant Bach: sleep little child. Songs taught by travelling minstrel before setting off to who knows where.

Tomorrow? Well that will be another day. People will come and go, earning a living, earning their keep. Children will learn and play and grow. Teenagers will itch to get away to a more exciting life. Meanwhile, life follows the rhythm of the seasons, pacing itself with the lull of time and the urgency of the moment.

There is much to do and eons to do it in. We have slowed down to a pace where healing the land means hearing the land. And healing community means listening beyond words. These are the tasks of transition. We relish the work, leaning in to it for the long haul.

Drudgery becomes meaning, urgency gives way to leisure, consumption to regeneration.

Hiding Brightness

The vanity of the technological fix is humanity's final act of denial. Virtually all our climate scenarios contain hidden within them some unknown, magical technology that will reverse the incessant stream of pollution we pour into the air. Elon Musk bets on giant spacecraft colonising Mars as the final solution. In the secret casinos of Wall Street the global mega-rich gamble hundreds of millions on creating virtual worlds where gullible customers can be their "true selves" in a non-existent shadow reality.

But you cannot run from your shadow side. You must turn to face it.

The global crisis is just that. The shadow side of human nature brought on by hubris and given fire-cover by denial. Our frantic efforts at infinite growth, to create wealth, to live in comfort, to tame the wild, all reflect aspects of our desperate modern psyche. Over the past five centuries we have built an economic system which has colonised the planet and now imprisons us in our darkest fears and deepest wounds.

To do more of the same, to bet on inventing technologies to save us, is folly. It is in the nature of the scientific-industrial-capitalist system that these technologies will have a greater overall environmental impact in their production than the positive impact they have in their use. This is in the nature of a system that externalises social and environmental costs. In a toxic system it is impossible to stay clean.

I grew up with sci-fi. I bought into the story that technology would bring an easy life, a galaxy of possibilities, the solution to every earthly problem. It has not turned out that way.

What's the human and environmental impact of the Rare Earths minerals used in our phones and the laptop I'm writing on? What about the cost of the electric car I now smugly drive around town or the PV cells that run my cooker? These things are hard to judge in the current system because their negative impacts are eliminated from the costs of the components. The planet and our future generations pay the cost.

The point is not that science or technology are inherently bad. It is rather that they are shaped by the civilisation they operate in and so cannot be fully trusted in a corrupt and decaying order.

What we know instinctively is that only nature can heal nature. It is planting trees that absorbs carbon dioxide, vegetation that slows soil erosion, manure that fertilises soil, hedgerows and forests that breed biodiversity. It is as simple as that. Hiding the brightness of human technology for a spell and replacing it with the drudgery of putting our hands in the soil will help to restore balance.

Hiding ourselves in common labour may also restore the balance in the human soul. Nature calms, physical work is meditative. Whether it's sewing, digging, planting, carving, the interaction between human creativity and a piece of natural material does something profound to the spirit. Cares dissolve, fire is quenched, inner power grows slowly and steadily fed by repetitive action. There is dignity in labour. There is growth in creativity. Wisdom is born in poverty.

Of course it is unlikely that humanity will elect to return to "The Dark Ages". We would be foolish to turn away from all we have invented. But we will need to be a little more discerning, a little more careful about the impact of both what we produce and how we employ it.

I'm told there is a difference between a tool and a machine. A tool is an extension of the human body or mind. With a machine we become an extension of it. This is where we lose our soul and become a cog in someone else's wealth creation. Having our spirit connected to the thing we labour on, wood, earth, wool, metal, water is what ensures our actions are creative rather than destructive. Regeneration and creativity are acts of communion.

Common labour, on common land, with common tools is the essence of the future world. For human life to survive and for all life to flourish, this cannot be a passing phase. This hexagram does not transform. It is eternal. In hiding ourselves in common labour we find profit and insight. The new story we are writing is one of creative interaction through head, heart and hand with the spirit of Gaia herself.

Embracing Drudgery

What world could we create? Eight billion sparks tripping electrical switches across the face of the globe. What could we imagine if we put our collective hearts into it? Released from the prison of wage-slavery, the oppression of materialism. Free to roam the wild edges of our collective imagination.

There is freedom in creativity, wild sexual energy harnessed by the bridle of the physical world. And there will be drudgery. The discipline that comes with bringing an idea to life, patiently tending it while it grows.

The resistance I experience in hearing the phrase "There is dignity in labour" means there is truth to understand in it. The dignity comes from taming the ego and subordinating it to the task of service. It comes from dissolving all sense of self-importance and entering into dynamic tension with a gang of co-creators. It arises from placing self in service of a greater need.

It is good for the soul. It calms the nerves. Microbes in the soil feed the gut, increase happy hormones in our blood, raise our spirits[xl]. We find calm amid the storm, in the simplest activities. There is meditation in knitting, mindfulness in turning the soil, deep reflection in brushing the hair of a child, a horse, an animal companion. In the smallest deeds we find the essence of human existence.

Our Revolution Begins with Food

In this period of the end of the world, how do we sow the seeds of a possible world? First, every young person should recognise that working with their hands and their hearts and their minds (and they are interconnected) is the highest evolution of our species. Working with our hands is not a degradation. It's our real humanity.

Start a garden. Create a playground in the way you grow food. Save seeds. Cook. It was treated as a backward activity that your mother cooked and was treated as not work. But she is the reason you are sustained. Start cooking classes. Get grandmothers to teach you.

Create communities. We are not atomised producers and consumers. We are part of the Earth family. We are part of a human family. We are part of a food community. Food connects us. Everything is food. And finally, never be afraid of deceitful, dishonest, brutal power. That is true freedom.

Vandana Shiva, Earth Activist[xli]

Brighten Yourself

The New Revolution asks us to reinvent ourselves. We must release the selves we have created from the material things we buy. We must let these false-selves crumble like the masks they are.

The New Revolution will involve finding a different way for us to define our identity, different from the clothes we buy, the car we drive, even the job we do. In the climax of the Age of Decadence, these things will suddenly feel empty and irrelevant.

So what will replace them?

Maybe it will be the deeds we do. We will be known for the gifts we give, that acts of kindness and community we perform, our artistic expression.

Maybe it will be the connections we develop: son of this, sister of that, creator of something, planter and grower of this and that.

Or maybe identity itself will no longer be quite so important. Maybe the need to distinguish myself from others will dissolve in the embrace of everything around me. What if the pursuit of non-identity becomes the path of revolution.

An Inspiration for Others

There is a contradiction at play when envisioning our possible future. Marx may be right that we only set ourselves such tasks as we can already complete. So we cannot imagine another world because we are stuck in an existing mindset. On the other hand, nothing will change unless we can see at least a glimpse of a different way of doing things.

Do we think ourselves into a new way of acting? Or act ourselves into a new way of thinking?

Maybe it's a bit of both. And maybe there's another factor at play: feeling. Imagination. Intuition. An innate sense of what's right, true.

When I let go enough of my sense of what's sensible and let my imagination free to roam amongst my wildest ideals, my strongest hopes and most foolish longings, I can start to see a different world.

It is a place without borders, where countries, customs and passports seem foolish and redundant. Instead communities are centred at a much more human scale. Villages, towns, city streets govern themselves in groups that are familiar, intimate and contain just enough of the diverse skills that are needed to survive. The magic number is somewhere between the Zone of Cooperation and the Zone of Reciprocity[xlii]. It is the size of a commune or a tribe – small enough to know everyone, large enough to get the job done.

Economies operate as networks, ecosystems of these communities each producing whatever they can, primarily for themselves but trading any surplus freely and reciprocally. The community is a Holon – both a self-organising, self-reliant whole and a part of something much bigger. It operates within a network of Holons, within a bio-regional Holon, within a geographic continent, within the world. Each reflects the qualities and attributes of both the bigger and the smaller entity in which it operates.

Enterprises are all self-managed, all not-for-profit, all purpose-driven. They create goods in common while stewarding the local environment in common. Nothing is done unless it leaves the earth better off than it was before. This is beyond sustainability and well into the territory of regeneration.

Life is no longer boxed off into time-bound chunks each of which divide the human spirit into irrelevant parcels. Learning takes place in the doing, in the communal activity of recreation and regeneration. Work is common endeavour – leisure and toil side by side, creativity and consumption two sides of a single coin.

And our roles shift with the seasons. Gardener in spring, weaver in winter, potter in the quiet evenings, song-smith or comedian in the lively nights. Sure, there is division of labour. Where expert skills are needed some folk specialise and dedicate their learning. But these roles sit alongside more generic ones where everyone mucks in in times of need.

It's a much simpler life. Less stuff, more relationships. Healthier because time is spent outdoors, relationships are more fulfilling, work keeps us fit. And there is plenty of scope for diversity. There are times to travel and experience, times to quest, to bring back new learning, new products, new food from far flung places. Times to find yourself, to create, to raise a family.

All energy is renewable, pollution a thing of the past. All farming is organic, human-made chemicals no longer valued or needed. Cancer has all but disappeared as the life-style and environmental causes (75% of all triggers by some estimates) are removed from our civilisation.

Transport, housing, food, clothing-production, goods and services, all have been made common again – run by community-owned, not-for-profit enterprises, allocated on a self-managed basis, arbitrated by the community only in extremis. In times of abundance the fear of scarcity, which pits us against each other dissolves into nothing.

Competition is replaced by collaboration as the driving force of life. Profit is similarly replaced by healing and regeneration as the life-purpose of the world. Attention is given to the new Holy Trinity of simple truths: a life of purpose, healthy relationships and creating abundance in nature. There is nothing more important than feeding these truths. They are the stuff that powers the world we live in.

In balance, these feed off each other: if I am balanced my relationships are healthy; if I feed the world around me it nourishes me and my community as a whole. In the sweet spot of this triumvirate lies the eternal life halfway between Heaven and Earth, a life of meaning, love, generosity, virtue. A timeless life longed for throughout human history. Shangri-la.

Idealistic? Of course. The world was never changed by being realistic. What's important is whether it feels true. Whether it chimes in your heart. Or soul. In the period when the wall starts to crumble we are allowed to be idealistic. In fact the times demand that we listen with everything we've got to the whispers of our heart's desires.

Coming of Age

This is the moment to define an age
the choice we were born into:
to follow ego's lust to the edge of loss
or turn to the lap of the land
let loose our grip on the reins of power
and slip instead into the step of Nature's rhyme.

This is the moment between mastery and trust
the decision to step from dominion into communion
to find our place not over but amid the fecundity
of a Universe on fire with love.

A world awaits.
It has sat quietly in the corner of your heart
the corner you've called childish, fantastical.
For years it whispered:
"I am real. I am already here.
That I beat in time to your blood,
that I sing in tune to your soul
is to remind you
of the part you'll play."
For years it has murmured
"Give in to the call
when this all gets too much.
To give in
is to let the yearning out,
to set free the timeless flow of human spirit."

For years it sang softly
to remind you that a world awaits
a world at one with itself
a world bursting with energy and love
a world too full of the fruits of toil

where dead seas and desert sands bloom
in infinite scent
where forests climb endless peaks
to breathe new life into rivers and skies
fields and shaded streets.
Imagine your place in it all
a home that feeds your soul
a role that does justice to every gift you hold
every dream you ever shaped
every simple act of kindness you forgot to make.

To love your neighbour
to nourish the soil
to share the bounty of shared endeavour
is not a childish game
it is a mirror held up to the human soul.
To tear down borders,
put need before greed
sew unity into every act
place first the healing of the Earth
is less a fantasy and more
the mission of a species understanding its worth.

This is the choice we came into
a delicious crisis that graces a race
once in its lifetime.
This is our coming of age.
Grab it while you can.

Deliverance Already Prepared

The future is here. But, as they say, it's just not evenly distributed[xliii]. Currently it's emerging at the margins looking for people, tribes, movements, bold enough to embrace it, determined enough to stick with it and creative enough to give it life. It's taking hold, drawing more and more folk into its orbit. But the pull isn't yet irresistible. Give it time.

The future is already here, but how to recognise it? How to see the whole when it's springing up in different places, growing, dying back, joining together into a shifting landscape? I have rewritten this section countless times, trying to capture the essence of a future just out of view: trying to see within the alternative movements of today the mainstream life of tomorrow. Trying to see the whole picture from the earliest shoots appearing above ground.

Let me borrow a framework from my friend Roberto Arrucha. Roberto is a man of boundless energy, a rather cheeky grin and a razor sharp intellect. I met Roberto in Vienna at a week-long workshop on supporting social enterprise to thrive. He was one of a group of non-Europeans who had found it difficult to break into the world of work in Austria. Seeing a host of social and environmental challenges they decided instead to innovate. They brought a very real energy, a determination and a focus on addressing real-world problems in a tangible and enjoyable way.

Rather audaciously Roberto has attempted to piggy-back on the UN's Sustainable Development Goals by crafting his own set of Human Development Goals. What he's come up with is simple but feels deeply true. For me it sums up a life well-lived. There are just three goals:

- A life of purpose
- Healthy relationships with others
- A respectful relationship with nature.

What better way to think of a future that's growing out of our deepest dreams and growing into the More Beautiful World we crave.

A Life of Purpose

Since returning home from Vienna I have stayed in touch with some of the young people who took part in that summer school. We meet monthly by video conference talking at depth about the issues and challenges in their lives.

They, like me, are wrestling with what to do with their lives in the face of a world of turmoil and impending destruction. The depth of the discussions leaves me in awe. I feel as if I'm sat in a room with the sages of old working out how to make sense of the modern world, how to bring meaning and service to the lives that lay ahead.

And these young folk are not alone. I have met the same sense of reflection and purpose at UN Climate talks, amongst urban working class youth, and amongst social innovators and activists. All are searching for meaning, examining their inner lives with care and attention so they can better impact in the wider world.

They are evidence of a New Spirituality that's taking root all around us. It shies away from the word God, conscious of the violence done in the name of religion. And yet it sees everything as sacred, to be cherished and protected.

It does not claim any particular lineage, happy to borrow wisdom from Buddhist scripts, indigenous peoples and local "old wives tales". Paying heed to the charge of cultural appropriation it honours the roots of these sources while claiming the fruits for the whole of humanity. If we are truly all one, in an interconnected cosmos, then what is sacred in one place or time belongs to the whole.

Its core tenets are the unity of all things, the sanctity of life, the thrill of being a part of creation. It embodies respect, curiosity, growth and reflection. Its aim is personal awakening in service of the greater good. Its students live with purpose treading lightly on the Earth, sensing the energy of those around them, equally at home in meditation, conversation or marching in solidarity with the cause of others.

It is a spirituality acutely aware of the coming crisis, the light and shadow of the human soul, the possible future that waits. It is intensely political without the dogma or agitation of Politics or Social Activism of the past, following instead the path of peace.

My world is full of activists who do not consider themselves to be activists. They are people doing what they feel is right, working to make their lives and their communities better. Their lives are filled with small deeds of kindness, altruism, community. They are artists, students, unemployed, social entrepreneurs, friends, brothers, sisters, parents. All guided by a sense of service and a sense of doing good without causing ripples along the way.

This new spirituality is the embodiment of our search for meaning, our felt-sense that there is more to life than selfish pleasures. The Long Arc of the Universe seeks out ways to consciously experience its own evolution. Our spirituality is one manifestation of this: the quest for understanding, meaning, connection to the underlying unity of all things, a felt-sense of the awe and wonder of being alive.

Healthy Relations with Others

Some say the human race can trace its line back to the San people in Southern Africa; perhaps are our oldest living relatives. A direct line to our original DNA. The San have been judged both the most egalitarian people in the world and the closest to nature (no coincidence there). They have no identifiable leader, since they surmise that to survive in their sparse and hostile environment everyone must know everything. Or they will perish.

This is the second transformational shift spreading across the world – the quest for new ways of organising ourselves that value everyone equally, allow all perspectives to be heard and that share work, reward and satisfaction.

In enterprises there are innovations like Holacracy, mutuals, cooperatives and Teal organisations. Many people are preferring the flexibility, innovation and freedom of start-ups rather than joining large corporations where they feel uninspired and unrecognised.

In social movements, Horizontalism has become the preferred way of operating, with its emphasis on consensus, group decision-making and shared power. Leading edge organisations are taking on peer working, distributed power and non-hierarchical structures that share responsibility and decision-making. In doing so they are learning how to avoid past pitfalls and shortcomings: the tyranny of the individual, structural power and paralysis in decision-making.

Across the world we're rediscovering the Council Ways, consensus and non-violent communication. We're developing tools to equalise participation, power and voice. We're also discovering that the process can be as important and valuable as the outcome, that hearing diverse views, valuing difference and hammering out difficulties is what ultimately builds community and cohesion.

This will shift the very fabric of our societies. Oppressions that are finely woven into our economic system will start to unravel – are already starting to. A system that has its historical genesis in colonialism, patriarchy and binary gender relations is already giving way to more fluid, more appreciative, more egalitarian forms of organising. Hierarchy and command and control are giving way to cooperation and collaboration as the driving forces of our community life.

All this will imply a different way to prepare people to be an active part in the unfolding of the new world. Listen to the dissenting voices in education and they describe schooling as a factory. They say it destroys creativity, that we are all born geniuses and education persuades us that only some are. Only a few succeed; the rest fail. They fail tests, they fail exams, they fail even to graduate from school. What kind of system is this? How does it help to develop grounded, rounded authentic adults?

Yet others say children spend too much time with other children. They do not have enough time with adults learning what it means to grow up. They are infantilised by education. Simultaneously, they are deprived of innocence and childhood in a toxic, over-sexualised, advertising-drenched culture of accumulation and waste.

The Unschooling Movement is imagining a world where children learn much of what they need to know by living embedded in a society, doing everyday tasks, learning important practical skills with adults, other children, older siblings and neighbours. Yes, sometime as kids, sometime as workers, sometime as learners, apprentices. Sometimes this might take the form of structured teaching sessions to convey core concepts and the Three Rs. Other times learning might be much more fluid and experiential. Horses for courses. The style of the learning environment reflects the content rather than a predetermined lesson format.

And this could go even deeper. The community of the future might not continue with the false dichotomy between consumers and producers. In the future world we will be both together. We will produce what we need, trade for what we do not have, live connected to the rest. Children will learn all this by doing. By being alongside. "Education" will cease, replaced by a life of learning and growth.

Beyond Restorative Justice

When a person among the Babemba tribes of southern Africa acts irresponsibly or unjustly, he is placed in the center of the village, alone and unfettered. All work ceases, and every man, woman, and child in the village gathers in a large circle around the accused individual. Then each person in the tribe, regardless of age, begins to talk out loud to the accused, one at a time, about all of the good things the person in the center of the circle has done in his life time. Every incident, every experience that can be recalled with any detail and accuracy is recounted. All his positive attributes, good deeds, kindnesses and strengths are recited carefully and at length. No one is permitted to fabricate, exaggerate or be facetious about his accomplishments or the positive effect of his personality.

Leonard Zunin[xliv]

Un-schooling the World

After visiting and working in many villages in Africa and India, I noticed that schooling was a vehicle for spreading industrial monoculture. It was like an AIDS virus which destroyed the immune systems of local culture, and local commons and local common sense. 'Educated' students became ashamed of their traditions and their elders, they became emotionally and spiritually disconnected from their fields and forests, they became useless members of their local economy. The entire backbone of community life was disrupted.

Alternative education means learning from Life, not from textbooks, exams and classrooms. So we got into all kinds of lifestyle explorations and projects such as slow food, zero waste, upcycling and design thinking, healing, community media, theatre, organic farming, natural dyeing, eco-architecture, etc. For all of our experiments, we made sure that we were the first guinea pigs. I have come to realize that if you want to do anything meaningful in life, you have to start by putting your own 'skin in the game'.

Swaraj University is India's first self-designed people's university where each learner (ages 17–28) could join and work on their unique dreams. We wanted to demonstrate that you do not need a formal degree to do well in life and we wanted to challenge the mainstream university. Two years ago, I helped start the Creativity Adda unschooling project in a local low-income government school with class 6–12 students in north Delhi, to show that these ideas of deschooling ourselves was possible across economic and social hierarchies. We wanted to challenge NGOs and social change agents to not be content with just throwing educational crumbs of the old system to the 'poor'.

We wanted to create a space where people who were aware of deep critiques of factory-schooling could come together and engage in creative ways to dismantle the educational monopoly and to regenerate diverse learning spaces and knowledge systems. We wanted to promote the idea that it was possible for people to learn on their own without the direction and structure of dominant institutions.

For me, unlearning has been an effort to decondition and de-institutionalize myself. Interacting with my grandmother led me to exploring and appreciating local sources of learning, traditional knowledge systems and the deep wisdom of village people. I started rethinking about all the things that I thought were 'dirty'. Waste and shit were the first things. I realized that my grandmother had no concept of waste. She was living a zero waste lifestyle. She would even upcycle vegetable and fruit peels into tasty dishes.

Manish Jain, India[xlv]

A Respectful Interaction with Nature

As the motor industry rusted away in its heartland of Detroit, people of colour moved to stave off poverty and hardship by occupying vacant land and growing their own food. The urban food security network spread like wildfire across inner-city USA. Not just fruits and veg, people experimented with fish farming and using the waste as fertiliser. Aquaponics was born.

Across the Atlantic a small town in the North of England took up the theme, using every available common space to grow herbs, organic veg and other food. Incredible Edibles in Todmorden inspired a movement of urban growing across the UK. The inspiration took root in unlikely places like post-industrial Middlesbrough. A declining steel and chemical shell, a shadow of its former glory, the city is now alive with people cleaning up the allies between their tightly packed terraces. These are being filled with planters, fruit trees, hanging baskets. Vacant land has been taken over as a People's Park where folk grow food communally. A group of refugees has taken over one corner of Albert Park and built raised beds next to the town's art gallery.

Meanwhile permaculture has become a global movement. People on every continent are learning how to design their lives and their spaces so that nature thrives, nothing goes to waste and energy is conserved. One step on from this, Eco-systems Restoration is using many of the same techniques and principles to actively restore landscapes that have been eroded by desertification, deforestation or over-farming.

This is not simply some kind of "nice to have" approach for a few lucky organic farmers. It is the very fabric of how agriculture and horticulture have been practiced at their best for thousands of years. And it's the way indigenous societies continue to grow food now. The approach of regenerative growing, leaving the land better than when you started, is also the very essence of addressing the world's ecological crisis.

In his ground-breaking assessment of the climate crisis Charles Eisenstein, whose work is echoed throughout these pages, cites research findings that attest to the power of healthy land stewardship:

*According to research at the Rodale Institute, if instituted universally, organic regenerative techniques practiced on cultivated land could offset over **40** percent of global emissions, while practicing them on pastureland could offset 71 percent. The potential for land-based CO2 reduction is over **100** percent of current emissions—and that doesn't even include reforestation and afforestation.*[xlvi]

At an even larger scale the bio-regional movement emphasises the importance of operating at a level where Nature's systems interlink to create an ecological zone of self-sufficiency.

All that is left is to rediscover the acupuncture points of the Earth's body that can bring the entire global eco-system, Gaia herself, back to full and thriving life. Maybe these are zones of extreme bio-diversity, maybe they are river systems, mangrove swamps or wetlands that process the blood and breath of the world. Maybe there are places where electro-magnetic energy pulses through the synapses of the Planet. Some say this was the purpose of the major sacred sites of old, places like the pyramids of Giza, and Stonehenge.

Return to The Commons

We are beginning to realise that the safest way to protect Nature is to return her to the Commons. Wherever people have lived in harmony with the land, at whatever time in history, it has been where there was no concept of private ownership of the natural world.

It is no coincidence that alternative movements are reclaiming the commons. They are occupying parks and squares, taking over vacant land to grow food, protecting water from fracking, pipelines and pollution.

In Brazil over a million and a half people are now members of the Landless Workers Movement which takes control of unproductive land turning it over to unemployed people. Across Europe and the US models like the Agrarian Trust are finding ways to buy up farm land as ageing farmers die out and to hold this in common for younger folk wanting to play their part in building a healthy regenerative food system.

And in Chiapas Mexico the Zapatistas have carved out an autonomous area where indigenous people and radicals run a parallel system of existence under the wary eye of a militarised Mexican state.

The World longs to be shared freely with all beings, to hear their chatter, feel their feet, experience the beat of their wings. We respond by stewarding the whole, guarding it for all life. Our affection for the Commons reflects our intuitive understanding that the World is too precious to be owned, too sacred to belong to any individual or corporation. It deserves to be enjoyed and shared freely with all living beings – human and non-human alike. The shadow arises when we step over the line of stewardship into ownership, believing that parcelling the world up is the best way to share it out.

Life in The Commons is how humanity has lived for the vast majority of its lifetime. Private ownership of the natural world is a modern construct designed to allow its exploitation and possession by a few.

To live in the Commons is to live in the generosity of the land and the community around us. It does not mean giving up boundaries or personal space but it does mean adjusting our sense of self, seeing where in blends into those around us. By all means keep your own front door, find the space you need to rest and reflect but know you are more the more you find your place in the wealth of The Commons around you. We are safer in the bosom of community than in the fractured isolation of rampant individualism and the patriarchal family. Hierarchy and power-over breed abuse. The Commons breeds community.

The economy of the future will be based on renewing and reinvigorating the Commons, not colonising and depleting it. This is the only way for human life to be regenerative. We are starting to see the first signs of this in movements such as Economy for The Common Good, the notion of Gross National Happiness and Regenerative Systems Design.

And there is The Gift. This is a return to the understanding that productive and affluent societies do not have to be based on bilateral transactions – me buying something from you. Instead I can offer goods or services to those around me knowing that in a Universe of abundance I will receive everything I need, not necessarily from you here and now but in due course thanks to the inherent generosity of life. Everything is produced from the Commons and given back to The Commons. We take only what we need, conscious of what we can pay, what others need and what's available.

Examples abound. Restaurants that offer food on a "Pay As You Feel" basis, the ability to "suspend" a cup of coffee so someone without cash can have it for free. Healers, coaches, freelancers who are prepared to negotiate their pricing. These are all examples of an emerging Gift Economy that is undermining the monolithic dominance of the capitalist market.

A Needs-Based Economy

The alternative to capitalism is a "Need based economy" or "Kemitism".

Capitalism stipulates that man is selfish and the only way for people to feel worthy is to accumulate properties or capital. Ownership of large property and capital is considered success, and ownership of little or no property and capital is considered failure.

Kemitism in contrary is a need based economy, whose philosophy is that all people have inalienable rights to land and natural resources on earth. Everything which is not created by humans, like land, air, water, and natural resources could not be owned and should be regarded as commons.

The community has obligation to make basic resources available to all members as a human right. The right to land is the first one. Right to habitat is second. The right to difference is third. And overall, Dignity is God's spirit in each human and cannot be sacrificed under any circumstances.

Ownership does not depend on precedence, entitlement or inheritance. Ownership depends on need and usage.

Land belongs to you as long as you need it and use it. A house belongs to you as long as you need it and use it. The moment you don't need and use a resource, that resources is endowed back to the community.

You cannot own what you don't need and use.

Land and natural resources belong to the community as a whole. They could not be owned or sold. Each member of the community receives resources depending on their need, and has access to all community resources depending on need.

One cannot be denied access to a resource which is not needed and used by other community members. Any resource not needed by the people, belongs to the community as a whole, and could be granted to new community members or foreigners.

Individuals are free to accumulate as much resources as needed by themselves. Extra resources accumulated should be shared in priority with family, then relatives and lastly with friends and strangers.

Laziness is a crime and punished by the lowest social status. Solidarity is the highest social value: "Ubuntu", expressed in the saying "I am, because you are".

That's the traditional African economical model.

Mawuna Remarque, Silicon Africa[xlvii]

A Common Treasury for All

Every single man, Male and Female, is a perfect Creature of himself; and the same Spirit that made the Globe, dwells in man to govern the Globe... therefore [s/he] needs not run abroad after any Teacher and Ruler... for he needs not that any man should teach him...

But since humane flesh (that king of Beasts) began to delight himself in the objects of the Creation, more than in the Spirit of Reason and Righteousness... then he fell into blindness of mind and weakness of heart, and runs abroad for a Teacher and Ruler... and thereby the Spirit was killed, and man was brought into bondage, and became a greater Slave to such of his own kind, than the Beasts of the field were to him.

And hereupon, The Earth (which was made to be a Common Treasury of relief for all, both Beasts and Men) was hedged in to In-closures by the teachers and rulers, and the others were made Servants and Slaves.[xlviii]

The Standard, by The Levellers, England 1649

THE COMMUNAL HOMESTEAD IN KELTIC BRITAIN
Among the Gaelic, or Scotch and Irish, and the Brythonic, or Welsh and Cornish, Kelts arable land was held and farmed in common, and this type of communal homestead, from Bosnia, represents well the kind which existed in Britain during the Keltic period. It was made up as follows: 1, common dwelling house; 2, summer dwelling house; 3, granary; 4, common goose-house; 5, cows' and goats' house; 6, shed for making plum brandy; 7, well; 8, common oven; 9, stables; 10, swine stall; 11, loft for maize; 12, paling; 13, maize; 14, orchard.

This picture hangs in the corridor at Canon Frome Court, where I now live. Its origin is unknown.

Restoring the Earth

We are living in a very important time for humanity. For thousands of years human beings have valued the things we make more highly than the natural systems that continuously renew the atmosphere, the water, the soil and the amazing biodiversity on the Earth. The consequences of this human choice have manifested as biodiversity loss, deforestation, desertification, toxic pollution and climate change.

We are experiencing the inevitable end of this cycle of ignorance and greed. The responsibility to understand and to restore ecological function on the Earth is arguably the most important task humanity has at this time.

Words can barely begin to convey the profound importance of what we are required to do. In fact, words, while necessary to communicate and educate, are not the solution. The solution is to physically engage everyone on Earth in the urgent task of restoring carbon in living soils, restoring vegetation cover to all areas where the soils are exposed and protecting and encouraging biodiversity in nature. Each individual's actions matter. Together our actions represent the collective human response to our historical failure.

We are all in this together. Every person, and in fact, all living things are affected by what has happened and by what we decide and do now. We can only change the situation if we all do this together. The Ecosystem Restoration Camps Movement represents a highly effective, low cost method to educate and engage everyone in the task of restoring the Earth. It also represents a way in which people are sovereign over their own future. The Movement is not only about restoring natural ecosystems it is also about restoring human rights and the rights of all life. It is about Freedom.

John D Liu[xlix]

What's Right in a Dark Time

We only ever met once but John Liu changed the course of my life. I don't think we even spoke. It wasn't John himself so much. It was more that the spirit of what John stood for shook my soul awake.

I watched John's documentary *Green Gold*, I read his articles, blogs and Facebook posts after we met. They knocked my socks off. Here was someone who had documented a way to reclaim the desert. He had given up his career as an NBC journalist to go to college to learn how to do it. And now he was setting up camps all over the world where people could gather together to regenerate degraded land. It seemed like a miracle.

As I dug further(!) I came to understand how regenerative agriculture was a movement emerging from permaculture and related fields(!) that was taking on seemingly hopeless landscapes and turning them back into fertile fields, forests and lakes.

I couldn't stop telling people about it. I was in awe. I had spent my whole life working on people – how we can grow, related more equitably to each other, support peace and here was a different world that seemed just as powerful. Perhaps more so. Part of me was immensely grateful to John and others for developing these immensely practical skills that would help heal the world. Part of me felt intensely inadequate – I hardly knew how to care for a house plant. Most of them died in my care.

And then at some point, I can't quite identify, I got bored of telling people about how awesome John's work was. I thought "If this work is so crucial to the future health of the planet, why don't you get on and learn it too. Surely the more the merrier?"

So I did. And it changed my life course. Actually I kind of cornered myself into it. Inspired by the urban farming movement in the US I came up with an outlandish plan to develop an eco-village in the heart of a post industrial town in the North East of England. When a local housing association came on board there was nothing for it. I had to learn regenerative horticulture or I'd have not a shred of credibility with the communities I was starting to interact with.

How had I got here from my distinctly ordinary former life: use, mortgage, children growing up in a comfortable market town, with a safe job?

Then things started to take a course of their own. Once I'd stepped into the stream I was washed along. I found a course in permaculture and took the summer of 2017 off to travel to Ireland for it. Sheila, my life partner came with me. We stayed on an eco-village in County Tipperary and saw first-hand what life in community, dedicated to the land could be like.

Returning home we looked at each other over breakfast one morning and discovered we'd both been harbouring the idea of moving into a community ourselves. In all honesty our motives were slightly different. Sheila was looking for the good life, a place to live more simply and learn the traditional skills of home, farm and craft. For me it was about being part of an experiment. I wanted a laboratory where I could learn the skills and approaches that would be needed to save the world: community, consensus, earth care, regeneration.

We gave ourselves a year to visit communities across the British Isles and find one we liked. Within seven moths we'd sold up, moved two hundred miles and moved into a house on a 40 acre communal farm populated by 45 other people.

When we moved in to Canon Frome Court in October 2018, the community had been running nearly 40 years. Everything ran like clockwork. There were rotas for everything: milking the cows and goats, feeding the sheep, collecting the eggs. there was a 2 acre Victorian walled garden split between all the households and run on a four year rotation system. We took up our plot and started growing squash and courgettes, harvesting them the next summer for everyone to share. That's how it works. We each farm our plot according to the rotation, sharing all we grew with anyone who wants it.

And it works. Mostly. Some food goes to waste, sometimes we run out of something we love, especially sweetcorn. Sometimes there are too many people on holiday at the same time, taking their kids away or running summer camps for other folks' children. But mostly we can manage all of these glitches. They are, after all what, make us human. How could we prefigure the future without them?

Many of our friends have called us brave for taking this step. It really hasn't felt like that. It has just felt like the obvious next step. Now we're here we're wondering why everyone doesn't live like this. Or nearly everyone. There will always be recluses, hermits, outcasts. And those whose egos cannot be managed even by an engaged community of critical friends. But for 99 out of 100, there are more benefits than not.

I'm still trying to work out what I've learnt from being here. I don't want to jump to early conclusions or try to distil 40 years of learning into a few trite lessons. It's too important for that. Yet I hear in my friends a curiosity to know how it is, an excitement to share vicariously in a life well lived.

And it has always been an experiment in "prefiguration" for me: if the current global order is heading irrevocably towards collapse, how do we start now to build the new world as the old one crumbles to ash.

I can't quite draw the conclusions, prescribe the lessons. All I can do so far is to describe the experience. It is much easier than I'd thought – both the living with others and the tending to Nature. I'm sure this is in large part because the heavy lifting was done years ago. We are benefitting from the efforts of several hundred folk who have passed through this community. Now all we need to do is slot into the rhythm of things – both human and natural.

And it has had a very tangible effect on my being, my soul. It feels slower, more intuitive. It feels like living in the land rather than on it. And there is a real ease about being with the same group of people, being interdependent upon them, working together on tasks, on a purpose. Bonds are growing across and between us, bonds of care, of delight, of respect.

I'm not sure how prefigurative we're being. I've almost forgotten that's why I came here. I've fallen into simply enjoying the days as they pass, moving between computer screen, vegetable garden, orchard and compost bin. Each action almost a meditation: cleaning bottles for the next apple juicing, taking care to sort and compost waste, tending squashes and picking raspberries. Is this prefiguration? Is it escape? Is it just the life I need right now?

Worthy Ideals

Inevitably the future will in large measure be determined by which aspects of the human soul are given room to breathe. Do we choose to feed the light or the shadow? And do we choose to demonise and repress the shadow or acknowledge it and treat it with kindness and reassurance?

Our current world has arisen out of the shadow of the human heart. It is built on pride, hubris, an over-inflated sense of human worth. It plays on the fear of insecurity, scarcity and competition. It is fed by greed and selfishness. And in the height of delusion it claims that all of this is human nature.

Human nature for sure but the shadow-side that arises under stress and fear.

There is another side, embodied by the movements currently taking hold at the margins, waiting to grow into an ecosystem of change to cultivate the barren soil. Those three Goals – a life of purpose, healthy relationships, respect for Mother Nature – reflect the deepest essence of what it means to be truly human – a human at peace with itself, at ease to enjoy life to the full.

The new spirituality reflects our deepest need for meaning and connection. The movement for egalitarianism arises from our innate sense of justice and our intuitive need to cooperate in order to thrive. The ecological restoration movement shows our boundless love for the Earth and our innate ability to conjure abundance from the world around us.

This is why these movements feel so right, so ideal, so true. Because they are alive in the very fabric of our DNA, waiting to be aroused by the hope of a different world.

6. Fording the Stream

What is the Best Way to Contribute to Global Transformation Right Now?

Already underway, the action has begun; proceed actively; everything is in place and in order. You are fording the stream of events. Everything is in the proper place and things are cooking. This is an advantageous situation and can bring profit and insight.

You can be successful through the small, through adapting to each thing and not trying to impose your will. Stay with the process.

Beginning things will open the way but trying to bring things to completion only creates disorder. Keep putting your energy at the service of what is underway. Set things right. You are in the right place. Carry on with the work.

[I Ching 63. Already Fording]

The Action Has Begun

I do not know whether I believe in reincarnation. What I do know is that the notion of reincarnation contains within it a stimulating thought-experiment. It goes like this:

What if we chose to incarnate here and now?

What if every single one of us knew in advance this was the moment of a massive, global human transformation?

Why then did we each decide to come?

What did we feel we could contribute - other than just to spectate?

What then is our unique contribution to this time? Why are we here, now?

In the Age of Decadence it can really feel like everything is going to hell. Especially if you follow the Main Stream Media. But something else is going on in parallel. Sometime around the turn of the millennium people started to notice that disparate interests groups were coalescing into an unstructured, unmanaged network of opposition to the global order.

Naomi Klein christened this the Movement of Movements. In his book of the same name, Tom Mertes tracked its early days from the indigenous uprising of Chiapas and the Landless Workers Movement of Brazil to the anti-globalisation protests of Seattle and Genova.

A group in Brazil organised the World Social Forum to give it a voice. A US observer, Paul Hawken started a database of organisations and groups that were part of it. This soon reached over two million entries before it became impossible to keep up to date. Hawken saw three main pillars of the movement: Environmentalism, Social Justice and Indigenous Rights. He describes the working of what he saw, like this:

"The Movement grows and spreads in every city and country and involves virtually every tribe, culture, language and religion from Mongolians to Uzbeks to Tamils... It provides support and meaning to billions of people in the world. The Movement can't be divided because it is so atomised – a collection of small pieces, loosely joined. It forms, dissipates and regathers quickly, without central leadership command

or control. Rather than seeking dominance the unnamed movement strives to disperse concentrations of power.[1]

As one global order descends into the Age of Decadence and Decay another process is already underway. Everything is in its right place. Things are in motion. How it will play out is up to us.

Seven mantras of the New Revolution

Change comes in waves, like the ocean, like sound, or ripples on a lake. Sometimes it's all action – Occupy, the Arab Spring, the summer of 1968. Sometimes it feels like nothing's happening, nothing's ever going to happen, no matter how hard you try. Or even that things are slipping backwards – like the sea sucking sand from under your toes.

Take a step back, and it's easier to see the overall direction of change. Our movement has been building since the 1960s when it swept across Africa and Asia as a torrent of national liberation struggles. Then came a second wave in the late '80s as the Berlin Wall fell and Apartheid came crashing down.

As the movement grew it started to find a new way of being. It took on the non-violence of Gandhi and King together with the mass mobilisations of Occupy and the Street Movements that flooded city Squares in the summer of 2011.

A movement needs mantras. Phrases that capture its spirit, focus its energy, help it concentrate on the task at hand. Our movement, which Naomi Klein calls the Movement of Movements, is no exception. As I move around, rubbing shoulders with Everyday Activists from across the world, I hear certain phrases repeated again and again.

1. The Revolution is Love

Deep in the soul of the movement we recognise that how we go about this revolution more and more reflects the world we want to create. It's no good pretending that means and ends are separate or that we can put off our principles until the day after tomorrow. No. We have discovered that we can act ourselves into the new world, here and now.

And because love is the driving force behind life, abundance, creation, the revolution is motivated by love. It embodies love. And there is no-one who is immune from giving or receiving love. Only love has the power to overcome the hatred and aggression of a system intent on destroying life itself – the kind of tough love that supports an addict into recovery.

2. We are Nature Protecting Itself

Witnessing the devastation wrought on the planet by an economic system that is out of control, we are moved to protect the world we love. At the same time we steadfastly refuse to adopt the notion of separation. Seeing humanity as separate and apart from nature is what allows the system to destroy the planet without a second thought. If we were "people" standing up to protect "nature" we would still be separate from it. No. We are nature's immune system. One part of nature acting collaboratively to protect the whole.

This is something we have learnt from Indigenous peoples who have been at the forefront of environmental protection since the advent of colonialism. From Chipko to Standing Rock and Idle No More, Indigenous movements, often led by women are protecting eco-systems and offering a glimpse of a life in harmony with the natural world. The rest of us are learning to re-indigenise ourselves, taking on the task of coming back into unity with the land, the water, the air. Anti-fracking groups in England are now seeing themselves as Protectors rather than protesters. This is our way to honour age old wisdom and decolonise ourselves, our lives and our shared movement.

3. We are the Secret World Government

When Charles Eisenstein first uttered these words at the New Story Summit in 2014 he named a deep truth. We are the new world government in waiting, a decentralised, human scale, earth-regenerating, life affirming, love-filled government. It would be government by the people for the people except that it is reaching further afield to embrace the vibrant living planet that holds us. Governance of Gaia by Gaia.

Those we see as having power are in reality constrained by the system they are part of. They have become functionaries in a corrupt and dehumanising system. They are only powerful for as long as we are mesmerised by the shadow of power they exhibit. Who wants that kind of power?

We know we have the power to build the new world, from the ground up. One act of kindness at a time. One relationship, one home, one street, one community at a time. This is the power of global transformation. The deeper its roots, the longer it will persist.

4. The Times Are Urgent. We Must Slow Down

Attributed to West African Elders this proverb reminds us that a clear head and an open heart are needed in times of chaos. The Movement understands this. It knows intuitively that its actions should not add to the chaos and turbulence. It understands that this mind-set of urgency and haste is part of the problem and so cannot be part of the solution.

Of course this creates an internal tension. A creative tension. We want to act. We know the importance of holding the line, standing firm, standing up for what's right. We also know that stillness brings new answers and a resolve of steel. It is out of stillness that the most grounded, compassionate and transformational actions arise.

But this is a self-aware movement. It has come to the conclusion that the dichotomy between spirituality and activism is false. So we approach our world-changing mission with the same centeredness we apply to yoga or music, tai chi, or painting.

One thing we've learnt along the way is that what you resist persists. What you embrace transforms. Which brings us to another dilemma. If we oppose the empire, we become the empire. Or to be slightly more accurate, we enter into a dynamic that gives it life and energy. Something tells us to stop fighting and try a different approach.

Erica Chenoweth's work on non-violence and non-cooperation gives credence to the strategies pioneered by Gandhi and King. Consistently across recent history it is non-violent strategies that have toppled repressive regimes. Remarkably she also found that it takes a surprisingly small number of dedicated, persistent activists to mobilise an entire populationli.

The Movement is full of folk who understand this dynamic. Pancho Ramos Stierle is one of them – a veteran of the Occupy movement in Oakland who was arrested while on a silent meditation protest. Pancho has a theory that of every ten revolutionary actions, nine should be about creating the world we want to live in:

> *Sometimes the most radical thing to do in a polluted violence-based system, is to be still. The mud settles to the bottom and we then have a clearer vision about our next steps... If we disobey with compassion and love in our hearts and minds, if we spend **90** per cent of our energy creating the alternatives of a just, free, and liberated world we will discover the joy to rebel against an imposed fear.lii (From Yes! Magazine.)*

5. Change Begins at the Margins

Permaculture teaches us that change does not happen at the centre. The core is the most stable part of a system. Change happens at the furthest reaches where outside influences come to bear, where diversity mingles and creativity flourishes.

The revolution will not storm the citadels of power. It tried that in the 20th Century and didn't much like the results. Instead it is growing in the wonderful, fertile actions of those who have abandoned the mainstream in favour of the experiment of prefigurative living.

The revolution is a living growing ecosystem. It's made up of the many and varied ways people around the world are putting into practice their wildest dreams of the good life. Like all healthy eco-systems it will grow and expand until it reaches a tipping point. The decaying remnants of zombie capitalism will be swallowed up and composted by the regenerative power of revolutionary yearning.

6. Everyone You Meet is Your Teacher

This mantra is the great leveller. It sees that everyone is of value and reminds me that I am always ready to learn and grow. If I see everyone as a teacher I become curious about them and open to lessons I did not expect.

Unlike past revolutions this one is the conscious liberation of the entire human race – not any single class or nation. This means integrating everyone into a single human family. No easy task for sure, especially during the transition when some will hold franticly to outmoded and dying ideologies. Fundamentalists will reveal themselves around every corner, even the ones we thought led to friendly streets.

How do we integrate things that we dislike or distrust? By asking questions: What is it like to walk in your shoes? What is this person who I see as an oppressor telling me about what's still needed to unite humanity? In what way is this person who annoys me a mirror held up to my face? What can they still teach me about my own rough edges, my shadow? And how can the movement be broadened to include their needs? After all, conflict is merely a human need that's going unmet. What human need do they represent? How can we make an ally of our former "enemies"?

There are no opponents. Only teachers and allies-in-waiting.

7. We are the Ones We've Been Waiting For

These are the words of an un-named Elder from the Hopi people of South Western USA:

You have been telling the people that this is the Eleventh Hour, now you must go back and tell the people that this is the Hour. And there are things to be considered...

> *Where are you living?*
> *What are you doing?*
> *What are your relationships?*
> *Are you in right relation?*

Where is your water?
Know your garden.
It is time to speak your Truth.
Create your community.
Be good to each other.
And do not look outside yourself for the leader.
This could be a good time!

There is a river flowing now very fast. It is so great and swift that there are those who will be afraid. They will try to hold on to the shore. They will feel they are torn apart and will suffer greatly.

Know the river has its destination. The elders say we must let go of the shore, push off into the middle of the river, keep our eyes open, and our heads above water. And I say, see who is in there with you and celebrate.

At this time in history, we are to take nothing personally. Least of all ourselves. For the moment that we do, our spiritual growth and journey comes to a halt.

The time for the lone wolf is over. Gather yourselves! Banish the word struggle from you attitude and your vocabulary. All that we do now must be done in a sacred manner and in celebration.

We are the ones we've been waiting for.

The Hoop of Life

Last week I was speaking at an event and I heard these words come out of my mouth: I am not compelled to speak as a woman, or as an indigenous person, a Diné tribal member. I am compelled at this time to speak on behalf of my species, as human being. I must answer for my kind now.

Some of you have heard me speak about the sacred hoop of life, that every life form has the honor of being given a place on this sacred hoop. Each family, plant, flying one, swimming one, creepy crawling one, four-legged one, two-legged one, must uphold its part of the hoop, or the integrity of the hoop begins to fail. We are a fiercely interdependent, inter-relational, "interbeing." Right now my kind, my species is not upholding its part of the hoop.

In "my section" of the hoop, there are really no distinctions of relevance: male, female, indigenous, "nonindigenous," rich, poor, intelligent, unintelligent, black, white, yellow, red, sane, insane, righteous, despotic, kind, cruel, spiritual, unspiritual. There is only the group known as "human being." Our effect on the hoop is the sum total of our actions as this group, all of us together. Our ability to maintain the integrity of the hoop is only as strong and effective as who we are as a collective. In this, we are bound together.

This realization has led to other surprising realizations. One that is arising right now is that never has it been so clear that my only option is to do all in my life to uphold the honor of being human being, to devote myself to remembering my perfect design for thriving life. This activity must consume all of my energy, Lifeforce, attention, willingness, ability. This means I must be willing to forgo other activities.

From this place, I understand that I cannot expect all injustices to be righted before I commit myself to Life. To wait until the injustices that I perceive touch me, my flavor of human being, to be corrected before I make this commitment to the honor of being human being, to Life, is beyond self-centered, beyond anthropocentric. It would be blasphemous to Life itself.

To engage in the infighting that is occurring within my species is fast becoming a deep insult on top of deep injury to all of the other members of the sacred hoop of life. While I insist on justice from "The Other" within humanity, all of the other children of the Mother Earth are suffering, fully at my kind's hands. This is not honorable. There is no Honor, or not nearly enough Honor, being upheld in this activity at this time. Not relative to Thriving Life itself.

Perhaps this is extreme thinking. Perhaps in order for my kind, my species, to be able to right itself into paying attention to its commitment to Life, it needs to answer for the acts of atrocity it has committed one to another. But perhaps not.

I feel that a part of upholding the Honor of being Human Being to me would be to allow for the possibility that I may have to forgo justice, as a woman, as an indigenous woman, as a brown person, and as all of the categories I am perceived to be a part of. I may have to forgo all the justice due to all of these categories, if I am to answer the call of Life fully, with all of my heart. I am examining myself and working to understand what it would take for me to be able to let them go and prepare myself instead, to look straight into the eyes of Life itself, and to hear what She wants of me and for me.

Pat McCabe (Woman Stands Shining)[liii]

Set Things Right

It may be that we can rely on the forgiveness and forbearance of the world's oppressed. It may be that they will follow the path that Gandhi and Martin Luther King set out for them. The path of radical non-violent civil disobedience – mass action based on both protest and the "Constructive Programme".

It would be convenient to think the noble peoples of the world, who have suffered five hundred years of colonialism, genocide and oppression will open their hearts wide enough to love their oppressor and in doing so they might crack the hearts of the world's demagogues.

We would be lucky if they heeded the words of Desmond Tutu:

When I talk of forgiveness I mean the belief that you can come out the other side a better person. A better person than the one being consumed by anger and hatred. Remaining in that state locks you in a state of victimhood, making you almost dependent on the perpetrator. If you can find it in yourself to forgive then you are no longer chained to the perpetrator. You can move on, and you can even help the perpetrator to become a better person too.[liv]

This is the path that will avoid conflagration. The path that rids humanity of hatred, anger and violence. But really, why should they? Is it really up to those who have borne the brunt of the past five centuries to let us all off the hook? Is it right to ask of any human being to forgive centuries of oppression based on dehumanisation, prejudice and exploitation?

But let's not fall into the trap of thinking only the wealthy and comfortable have the luxury of enlightenment. This is the ultimate indulgence of privilege. Justice, forgiveness and compassion are not the preserve of the rich and leisured classes. This is pious non-sense. They are the essence of all humanity. We all have wounds to heal, wrongs to forgive, opportunities to rise above our shadow and display our better self.

Why would we want to rob each other of this gift?

Already There

The old story has finished
I have felt it for a long time.

Connect with Earth as a place of Mystery and Meaning.
Be fearless in knowing that
      Being is as powerful as doing
      Reflection is the perfect teacher
      Change comes from subtle actions tenderly offered.

Our journey is love and kindness to all beings
The first step is knowing self
      Being passionate
      Reaching out to others holding a different mind-set
      Feeling comfortable in storylessness.

I have decided to give the whole of me
I'm not hiding anymore.
I will relish the noise I can make.
From now on, there will be more dancing!

Collective Poem

Begin Things

The task of our age is not to bring an end to global capitalism. It is not even to create the final blueprint of the New Order. It is simply to begin things. It is to innovate, create, prototype. The grand design of a new way of being is beyond human wit. It is only by acting our way into it that we will find the new story.

So let's begin things. Let's relish in unbridled human creativity. Let's invent a new world one small step at a time.

Thinking there is a grand plan, trying to imagine it all, plan it all, strategise, is all part of an old mind-set. That's another version of the old story. Anyone who tells you they have a plan, that they already have the answer is living in the past. Beware their ego, it will betray you.

There is plenty to do. Plenty for us all to occupy ourselves with. We will need a new way of doing everything. Raising the young. Ensuring the physically impaired are central, important, included. Caring for the old. Growing food. Making a living. Caring for the land. Valuing diversity. Sharing the bounty of the Earth. Producing the things we need. Cleansing the water. Closing the circle to make waste obsolete.

These are the tasks we are starting to set our minds to. These are the tasks that will occupy the future. The task is to begin these and other endeavours, guided by the most generous and beautiful aspects of the human spirit. Forget finding the answers. Forget creating a complete new system. That will all evolve in time.

This is an eco-system evolving, growing, spreading to cover the face of the earth with abundance, radiance, growth. You do not plan a new form of human civilisation on a spread-sheet or project map. You caste seeds, nurture shoots, find the things that feed each other, are companions, work symbiotically.

Begin things. Join the revolution. Start where you are. Start anywhere, follow it everywhere.

Things Are Cooking

It's in the nature of things that the new grows within the old, starting at the margins where the grip of convention is lighter, where the disaffected and radical hang out. It grows inward, creeping under cover of night, feeding on the ashes and decay of the old, until unnoticed it has spread to the centre.

It is in the nature of human innovation that it never starts in the strongholds of the status quo. How could it? Change always starts first at the margins. It simmers away here until it is well-cooked and the aroma begins to spread, calling in others. When enough are attracted a shift begins. A tipping point has been reached.

To succeed, two things usually happen. The first is crossing that tipping point. This is trickier than it seems. Change at the margins attracts outsiders, people who love to be different. A tipping point requires at least some of the silent majority, the more conventional. This means the outliers have to change the message to attract the majority. They have to make the new way normal rather than alternative. Plus, at least some of them need to hang around long enough to embed the change, rather than moving on to new horizons.

Second, it seems change goes through phases. From emergence, excitement, structure-less-ness to order, organisation, action. And then back again. Back and forth in a creative dance. Chaos, order, chaordic exchange. To stay too long in either mode will kill the onward growth.

Get these things right, simmer the pot for long enough, grow the eco-system from the edges in and we can colonise the decaying system and decolonise the world.

Success Through Small Things

If we look hard enough we can see all around us the faltering baby steps of a new world walking blinking into the first rays of morning sun.

There are moments that act as a lightning rod for the more beautiful world. The falling of the Berlin Wall, the Unknown Professor standing with his shopping bags in front of the tanks in Tiananmen Square, Mohamed Bouazizi setting himself on fire and sparking the Arab Spring. They are moments within a tinderbox atmosphere where a single spark can ignite possibility.

Standing Rock became an almost magnetic attractor for these moments. One came when veterans from each of the US Armed Forces joined together to ask for forgiveness for the genocide perpetrated against indigenous peoples[lv]. In another, representatives of US Churches apologised for the Doctrine of Discovery which had provided religious cover for this genocide.[lvi] These are the moments that heal the divisions within humanity wrought by a system of greed, extraction and materialism.

How do we nurture more of this? More of these sublime moments. When the young woman protester brings the militarised cop to tears? When the skin-head poses for photos with the Black Lives Matters dad, so he can show his kids? When the holocaust survivor in her nineties forgives the Nazis because she does not want the hatred to consume her soul before her death?

What would that feel like, if humanity stepped from ego to eco, if the world bent itself towards love, abundance, connection. What an amazing place this would be to live. What if we dipped our toe into the Long Arc of change and felt its presence from source to ultimate surrender and all these moments in our lives in between. What if we remembered the future version of ourselves that we already are? It's not so far from here to there. These moments are all now.

Healing the Ills of the Ancestors

We have work to do. A prime directive. This is part of the reason we have come into the world – to make right that which others who preceded us failed to do. And to get to that level through a collaborative journey with the Ancestors. Excluding them limits our capacity to encompass the issue with the kind of imagination we need. This is why we need the ancestors to broaden the scope of our imagination enough to address this issue of separation, isolation, disruption...

In my tradition we say we become a lot wiser, a lot more advanced in our consciousness when we cross into the other dimension. We have to realise that compassion is key to a better understanding that shows these ancestors where they had failed when they were in this world.

This perception leads them to long for a deeper connection with those they pass on the baton to – so that together, through a collaboration the ill that they did simply because of the circumstances they were in, can be repaired.

Those who have a misgiving towards the ancestors, should sit with them and communicate to them how it feels. The ill that they committed must be communicated back to them as a way of demonstrating that we are now aware, because we are dealing with the consequences of their actions. Those actions cannot be transcended without their practical presence, inspiration and guidance.

We can't just pray to the ancestors in a simple fashion as if nothing had happened when we are living the consequences of their actions. It is a way of creating a healing across the great divide. Healing for the ancestors and healing ourselves. Which is why our task is so important and so big, lest we end up living a life of resentment and victimhood. That has nothing elegant about it.

Dr. Malidoma Patrice Somé – Dagara Elder, Burkina Faso.[lvii]

Occupy God

Capitalism has colonised God. It has turned the universal spirit that moves through all things into a superhuman deity, punitive father, defender of patriarchy, friend of the rich, instigator of war, famine and injustice.

The dynamics of commodification have crept into every nook and cranny in the temples of religion. By this I do not just mean that spirituality is being bought and sold, packaged up into books, trinkets, experiences that are crowding into the market place of human liberation. Although this is certainly the case, especially in the US.

There is something even deeper at work here. Commodification drugs us into thinking the answer to our every problem is in buying a product or buying into a lifestyle or an allegiance. Our identity and with it our path to liberation lies in the things we attach ourselves to. By its nature, this implies that "solutions" to "problems" come from outside. They are external to us. Separate from the thing we call "self".

This is the real impact of our global order upon spirituality. It has turned spirit from something integral, in, out, through, into something external. Something to be mediated by preacher, priest, guru, imam, spiritual teacher. From a personal journey of growth and discovery into something to be bought from someone wiser or more advanced than us.

Capitalism has occupied God, colonised the spiritual. It has taken wisdom and peace of mind, something intrinsic that I can achieve, refine and develop and turned it into a set of superhuman characteristics embodied in an external all-powerful God or teacher.

This shift disempowers me, encourages me to look to others for answers, to look to God for guidance or salvation – instead of working with my peers to realise my own highest potential and finding the wonder of the evolving universe within me as within everything in the living cosmos. I go from searching for unity to waiting for instruction.

As the old story falls apart and people find within them the capacity to follow their own spiritual path, we open up a new possibility. We open up the possibility to take back spirituality from priests and gurus and from an externalised anthropocentric God and to find instead the sacred in everything. Every rock and grain of sand. Every bug and tic, spider, bird, slug, snail, fish, and frog. Every tree and bush, flower, leaf and blade of grass. And in ourselves and everyone we meet.

This is the difference between spirituality and religion. This is the fruit of decolonising God, reoccupying spirituality. It is taking spirituality out of the church, temple and synagogue and placing it in every house and street, river, valley and stream. It is seeing the sacred in oneself and seeing oneself as the sacred in everything else. It is reclaiming spirituality from the dying grip of a host of patriarchal religions and giving it freely to the world, where it belongs.

This is a deeply revolutionary process. Together science and religion forcibly removed the sacred from everyday life. They murdered the local guardians of sacred rituals, natural medicine and healing – the witches who held a special place in every village across Europe. They tried also to kill it off in the indigenous cultures they colonised. In doing this they tried to colonise spirituality and called it religion.

Reclaiming spirituality is a process of liberation, re-indigenisation, decolonisation. It is a return to the intrinsic human state – one that replaces materialism, vanity and selfishness with connection, love and joy.

The Divine Collective

The Buddha Shakyamuni predicted that the next Buddha would be Maitreya, the Buddha of love....

It is possible that the next Buddha will not take the form of an individual. The next Buddha may take the form of a community, a community practicing understanding and loving kindness, a community practicing mindful living.

And the practice can be carried out as a group, as a city, as a nation.

Thich Nhat Hanh, Vietnamese Zen Master

Crisis

From the ancient Greek for a decision. Not so much a place where everything is in chaos but more a time when a decision is calling to be made.

Often this is presented as a bifurcation – a choice between two opposing futures. In our era, the choice between authoritarianism and liberalism, between fear and control on the one hand and love and acceptance on the other. One leads to a future of repression the other to peace on earth. The age old battle of good and evil.

Yet something tells me it cannot be as simple as this. If the future is to embrace the whole of humanity, living together as one, it must have a place for both love and fear, control and acceptance. Our fear after all, is only our ego speaking to protect us. Control, the desire to bring order from chaos. They sit alongside love and acceptance. If anything they must be processed before we can find peace. We find in the space after fear has been acknowledged, not in its rejection.

This autumn I met a young Italian women called Lisa. She perturbed me more than a little. One evening she confessed that she had made a list of her favourite dictators. She had studied them all and categorised them according to the degree of control they exerted, the level of violence in their regime and the relationship between the two. I could not work out if she revered them or feared them. Or both.

I ventured a view about the global crisis – that it represented a tussle between people motivated by control on the one hand and those motivated by love on the other. The former were found amongst the supporters of dictators and Authoritarian Populist regimes the world over; the latter in the alternative left, the Movement of Movements seeking change.

This characterisation did not sit well with my young companion. She did not want her desire for order to be characterised as reactionary or Fascistic. When we unpicked this a little more, we both came to understand that without people like Lisa, who live to establish order, there would be no future. This is not an impulse to be confined to the dustbin of history but rather an archetypal impulse that settles a society and that will play a crucial role in the new world civilisation.

No matter how counter-intuitive it felt, I have to admit it felt important to embrace even those who most strongly see the need for some sense of control. The crisis is not a battle between good and evil, love and control. The path to the next order will not be taken by the victory of one side over the other. It is more about the resolution of the two. The integration of change and stability. The symbiosis of love and order. For both are integral to human nature.

7. An Arousing Shock

What Stages Will the Transformation Pass Through?

Do not get caught up in things. Free yourself from anger, lust and hatred or greed for gain. This can bring a new time. If you do not correct yourself however, you will continually make mistakes through ignorance or faulty perception.

Action now is inspired by the spirit of heaven. Proceed like this, step by step. If you do that, success will be your fate. If you become entangled and lose the connection, how could you do anything right.

Inner growth remains free of entanglement through its continual connection to heaven.

This is a disturbing and arousing shock, a burst of new energy. It brings new life and new love. Rouse things up to new activity. Re-imagine things. Let this shake up your old habits. When it first comes the shock is frightening. Then joy and laughter soon follow. Do not get carried away. Focus on offering something to the spirits who have given us this joyous life. Act as the master of ceremonies that bring fertility back to earth.

[I Ching 25, Without Embroiling, transforming to 51, Shake.]

Action Inspired by Heaven

The New Revolution is not about bringing down the system. To fight the system is to become locked in the system. To fight requires you to take on the mind-set of the paradigm you are trying to shift. What you resist persists.

Once we understand the nature of time and change and the history of empires, we understand that we do not even need to bring down the system. This will happen of its own accord. It is written in the DNA of the system itself. It will die under its own weight, consumed in its own shadow.

What's at stake, the question of our age is which path we choose to take. To fight the current order continues us along the same path. And it's not necessary. Once we internalise the knowing that the system is

doomed, the task of the future become one of nurturing the new order. This is the second path. The path of growth, life, truth, abundance. The green path.

All that's needed is to live the life we dream of. Not as individuals pursuing their selfish passion, but as communities, villages, streets, groups of friends working together to create the communities of the future. By tirelessly focussing our energy on the future we build it from the ground up. We call it in, create the space for it to grow.

By following the green path we clear it for those behind. And we avoid perpetuating the chaos of the end of days. We deprive the dying system of oxygen. We stop buying into its fallacy of perpetual growth. We take ourselves out of the system and create a new parallel new one.

And because this is the future, the tide of time is on our side. We do not make the future. It is already present. The best we can do is clear the space for it to move into the present. The world is opening the space, Gaia is calling it in. We can write the tune that brings it in. We can create the rituals that guide it home.

Getting Caught Up in Things

At this point in the process I was in a state of bewilderment. I had lost much of what I believed to be true. The accepted wisdom of revolutionary change was, according to the I Ching not going to help us through the coming transformation. Imposing the will of a revolutionary vanguard would be suicidal. Conflict between power blocks would bring us to the edge of death. Crisis would follow any transformation, stretching systems to breaking point. Utopia is postponed.

And there was no bright technological future. It was small things, drudgery, that would bring life back to a dying planet. Seeds, soil, children, getting our hands dirty. Sweat and toil. Looking back, I see I was resistant to much of this – for a while at least, before I let it settle in. Before the writing helped me to etch its truth into my bones. Still, it was I challenge. The part of me that needs to know, that needs reassurance, wanted more answers. How close was the transition? Was it a point or a process? What stages might it go through? Where do we even start and how do we keep going?

I returned to the I Ching to unpack this last Reading, Without Embroiling. What on Earth did it mean? Surely there was more to be done than just freeing ourselves from anger and greed? How could this dismantle a global system of profit and accumulation that had lasted five hundred years and was steadily devouring the planet, immune to all our efforts at change?

Delving deeper revealed four Steps of Change. Four processes within the global transformation that will unfold ahead of us. In addressing the question about how the transformation would unfold, the I Ching starts at 25 (Without Embroiling) and moves to 51 (Shake). There is a way to track this change from one shape to another. It reveals two intermediary steps, so four in all. I imagine this process is based on an ancient understanding of the way change happens, the flows of energy through the Universe. I hope it is based on an innate understanding of the shape of The Arc, its graceful lines and the stars it cuts across.

1. **Without Embroiling**: proceed step by step. Free yourself from anger, lust, greed and hatred. Do not get caught up in

things. Be guided by the spirit of heaven or you will continue to make mistakes.

2. **Gnawing and Biting Through**: You are confronted by a tough obstacle. Gnaw away, be determined until you bite through. Take decisive action. Use law and punishment where necessary. Insisting on your rights and going to judgement will bring profit and insight. Your determination can break through obstacles and shed light on the situation.

3. **Following**: You are drawn forward by a strong attraction. Follow the inevitable course of events. The call has come. Let go of what is past. Be guided by the way things are moving. The whole world must follow the times and seasons. You are following a righteous idea inherent in the time.

4. **Shake**: This is a disturbing and arousing shock. A burst of new energy. It brings new life and love. Rouse things up. Reimagine them. Shake old habits. At first this is frightening, then joy and laughter follow. Do not get carried away. Focus on offering something to the spirits who have given us joyous life. Act as a master of ceremonies to bring fertility back to the earth.

Once again, in this Reading, I lost pieces of my world view. Instead of starting with political strategy, the process begins with an almost spiritual cleansing. Then we are encouraged to use all the mechanisms possible within the existing order, to challenge its own foundations. This felt like reformism par excellence. Surely this would get us no-where. You cannot use The Master's Tools to Dismantle the Masters House. Or so I'd been told.

We are being tested here. Asked to truly become the change we wish to see in the world. First we rid ourselves of anger and hatred. Then use all the legal and constitutional means at our disposal. Then follow some ethereal call, the inevitable path of a righteous ideal. Then things will be shaken up – almost despite everything. As they are, we are asked to engage in ceremony with the spirits, calling them to bring fertility back.

I can't be sure if the four Steps of Change follow sequentially or if they overlap. At the time of reading they made little sense to me but as time has gone on, I see more of them arising. Four steps to move us through collapse, crisis and beyond. Four steps on the path to the New Earth. Four steps that fly in the face of the orthodoxy of social change, inviting us into a deeper flow of evolution.

Free Yourself

In my lifetime there have been three times when the winds of change have swept across the face of the earth, stirring up dust, shaking old regimes to the ground, blowing fresh air into dark places.

The first was the 1960s. It did not start with the hippy movement and the summer of love. This was where it ended. It began in Africa with an irresistible call for an end to colonial rule. It moved from there to Vietnam and the war for liberation from French and US rule. This shook the colonial powers causing waves of sympathy and solidarity amongst the youth. Paris, San Francisco, Montgomery, Harlem were alight with anger, protest and possibility.

The second wave came in the mid 1980s with the fall of the Berlin Wall and the collapse of the monolithic, state-dominated socialism of the Soviet Bloc. Here too there were echoes across the world – struggles against military dictatorships in Latin America and Asia. Each time the world watches, waits and often takes the chance to bolt for freedom.

Wave three started in 2011, the year of Occupy and the so-called Arab Spring. Everywhere people took to streets and squares to find what was emerging in this time of turbulence.

A new lens entered the public discourse. It was the lens of the 1%. It sought to convince us that humanity was united, had common interests, hopes, dreams. All except for a tiny minority – those who held on to power and wealth at the expense of the rest of us:

> *We condemn the current distribution of economic resources whereby only a tiny minority escape poverty and insecurity, and future generations are condemned to a poisoned legacy thanks to the environmental crimes of the rich and powerful. "Democratic" political systems, where they exist, have been emptied of meaning, put to the service of those few interested in increasing the power of corporations and financial institutions.*

> *The current crisis is not a natural accident; it was caused by the greed of those who would bring the world down, with the help of an economics that is no longer about management of*

the common good, but has become an ideology at the service of financial power.

We have awakened, and not just to complain! We aim to pinpoint the true causes of the crisis, and to propose alternatives.[lviii]

The whole point of these street movements of 2011 was that they had no leaders. The crowd was in charge, stretching its muscles, hearing its own voice repeated in call and response because megaphones had been banned. It was a time for the mass to imagine horizontal rule, to debate and agree all things by consensus.

Within this dogged devotion to anonymity there were moments of renown. In one of these, Pancho Ramos Stierle reached cult status in the Bay Area Occupy movement. Pancho, an undocumented Mexican activist, was arrested by Oakland Police while meditating. When spirituality is placed in service of system change it becomes a crime in the eyes of the status quo.

On Mondays we practice silence, and the police officer who arrested us thought that we were deaf because we were not speaking. So he got a notebook and a pen. It was very considerate of him, and I could feel his energy shift a little, and so when he gave me the notebook I wrote, "On Mondays, I practice silence, but I would like you to hear that I love you."

When he read that, he had this big smile and looked me in the eye and he said, "Thank you. But, well, if you don't move, you're going to be arrested. Are you moving or not?"

So I wrote back, "I am meditating." He said, "OK, arrest them one by one."[lix]

A student of non-violent direct action, Pancho sees the emerging social movements as a blend of spirituality and activism:

It is time for the spiritual people to get active and the activist people to get spiritual so that we can have total revolution of the human spirit. Because we have the idea that the self-indulgent people are just meditating—they are going to caves and meditation centers while all this madness is happening, or you have people at the meditation center that are asking how can you bring peace and calm and harmony to the world if you do not have that in your heart?

I think that we need both now, and that we need to combine this inner revolution with the outer revolution to have the total revolution of the spirit.

Then you can build the alternatives to a collapsing system built on structural violence.

I believe that nine out of ten actions must be creating the community that we want to live in—we're talking about permaculture, independent media, restorative justice, gift economies, free currencies, and preventive medicine. By doing all that, we make ourselves stronger.

Some say that Occupy failed, that the Arab Spring fell apart and allowed the military back into power. At one level this may be true. Zucotti Park was cleared of protesters. In the Middle East governments came and went, some states were recaptured by the military, others were left in chaos. The democratic high was followed by the inevitable come-down.

The argument goes that the protesters were naïve, had no clear platform, did not know how to take and wield power. One of the instigators of Occupy Wall Street, Micha White looks back on the experience from this point of view:

Occupy was holding assemblies in public squares to create a consensus-based democracy that we hoped would give us broad social legitimacy. The thinking was that, if every day people convened in these democratic assemblies, the police wouldn't be able to attack us because we would be the sovereign power.

Well, we realized that that's not true. Actually, sovereignty, in our societies, is only given to the people who either win elections or win wars. Winning wars isn't possible or desirable. Winning elections actually seems like something that can happen.[lx]

At another level, this analysis misses the point. It takes us back into the existing paradigm of politics, where money and power rule. The idea behind these street movements was to prototype a new form of politics by creating space for emergence.

This is what made it a Presencing movement. By holding to the importance of process, by resisting the urge to find easy answers, Occupy was asking what the future was calling for. It was a glorious fleeting attempt to hold society at large in the liminal space of not knowing.

Many of those directly involved saw the movement as valid in its own right. It was a glimpse of how the world could be organised, an experiment in mass democracy, mutual support, deeper understanding.

And some feel it has spawned a new, more spiritual form of change-movement:

This new spirituality is about doing something to help the world in a way that requires sacrifice rather than being spoon-fed easy answers. It is about discovering your true calling, your unique gifts and offering them... in service of compassion and justice.[lxi]

You may share this sense of emerging spirituality. You may not. That's not really the issue. What this trend points to is a rediscovery of simple wisdom – deep and old knowledge about how to live in harmony with those around us by simultaneously living at peace with oneself. Inner and outer balance.

A Call to Arms

Somewhere there is a photograph of me brandishing an AK47. I am in a straw hut on a sunny Ethiopian morning, having narrowly escaped death in an air-raid the previous day. It is 1986, a few days after my 23rd birthday and I have come to the Ethiopian countryside in search of revolution.

As a guest of the Tigray People's Liberation Front I am in rebel-held territory in the middle of a bitter civil war that has both arisen out of and in no small part contributed to the largest famine the world has seen in decades. Nearly half a million people are dying – some from famine, others from widespread human rights abuses at the hands of a brutal Soviet-backed dictatorship.

While Bob Geldof harangues the British public about saving starving African children, I have taken a different path. I had heard about the war of liberation against the "Derg" and the inspirational changes that were happening in the liberated zones. This was revolution in practice. So when the chance comes to visit, I jump. Neither my mother nor my wife of two and a half years are much impressed by this decision.

What I find is indeed inspirational – land redistribution, people's councils, women's groups and a whole host of ingenious ways to make the most of a dirt-poor situation. Drunk on these advances and full of the heady ideals of youth, I am living out a fantasy of the romance of armed struggle.

These fighters are the warmest, most comradely people I have ever met – passionate about their cause, committed to human liberation, selflessly devoted to each other. They study political texts, walk hand in hand and are guided by simple egalitarian principles: "do not borrow so much as a pin from the peasantry", "swim amongst the people like a fish in the sea".

I learn their revolutionary slogans and delight their meetings by repeating them in local dialect: "All power to the people" and my personal favourite "Without women's liberation there is no social liberation".

My colleague Jenny Hammond and I tour Northern Ethiopia drinking it all in with wide-eyed wonder. We meet all the rebel leaders including

Meles Zinawi, the man who would go on to become Head of the Ethiopian state for two decades.

Looking back with the benefit of age and the knowledge of how it all turned out, I do not know whether I really believed that armed struggle was the answer to repression and inequality or whether I was simply romanticizing a world far removed from my own comfortable middle-class Western life.

At the time it felt as though only armed revolution was capable of overthrowing a system that seemed to hold all the cards and wield all the power. It was commonplace to believe that the rich and powerful never give up privilege without a fight. It seemed as though Malcolm X was right – that it would take "All means necessary".

There appeared to be examples where this had succeeded. The African Liberation struggles of the sixties for example – where armed uprisings had brought an end to European occupation. Then there was a smattering of other revolutionary countries such as Nicaragua, Cuba and Vietnam. It was revolutionary orthodoxy to believe in the armed struggle – this is what made you a revolutionary.

It was as though the radicalism of the means was more important that the radicalism of the outcomes. It was the way to prove you really meant it when you said you were a revolutionary. We had forgotten, or perhaps never realised, that means shape ends.

There is an unspoken sixth feature of the Global Transformation Movement, which is taken for granted by the movement. It is based on non-violence. Whereas many of the social movements of the Sixties made a feature of non-violence, the Movement of Movements have integrated it so fully that it is unspoken. The youth in Occupy were not so much practicing non-violence as just wanting to model a new way of organizing society and wanting to be left alone to do it. When this became impossible they worked tirelessly to respond to hostility and oppression with loving kindness.

We sometimes think of non-violent resistance as an Eastern invention, coming from Gandhi and adopted by Westerners returning from pilgrimages to India. In truth, non-violence has been round the world and back, perhaps several times. Martin Luther-King championed its use in the US. King was inspired by Gandhi who in turn credited Tolstoy, a Russian, who in turn was inspired more generally by John Ruskin, a Scot. All this while, more often than not, it has been women in the vanguard of non-violent practice since as far back as Lysistrata's character in the Ancient Greek play by Aristophanes.

Veteran US campaigner Gene Sharp has taken King's legacy of non-violence back out around the world. He's been credited with helping to inspire non-violent revolutions in a number of post-Soviet states and elsewhere – so much so that some have accused him of being a CIA stooge.

Sharp has analysed dozens of countries where the people have overthrown a dictator, together with other struggles such as trade union disputes and civil rights movements. He has carefully documented how these struggles succeed through applying careful strategic planning and flexible tactical methods. In his works Sharp identifies a total of 198 techniques for non-violent struggle from around the world[lxii].

For me the list is comprehensive but somehow fails to capture the full creativity of possibility. In truth the methods of nonviolent action are as wide and tall as the human imagination itself. They are every act of kindness, non-compliance, rebellion or disruption we have ever imagined, that refuse to come from a place of conflict. To confine the creativity of revolution to a mere 198 methods feels like trying to list the ways you might admire a sunset.

Nonviolent struggle has been waged ever since people felt their leaders had become detached from reality. It has embodied the most creative and imaginative form of protest and opposition. More often than not, women have been at the forefront. From The Mothers of the Disappeared, to the women's peace movement at Greenham Common to the Chipko movement protecting forests in India, women have inspired movements that have stood the test of time.

If Gandhi and Sharp provide the Yang of non-violence then a rich legacy of women's groups provide the Yin. At its best this archetypically feminine way offers an organic, communal approach that is powerful in its ability to withstand oppression while holding true to a vision of how people can organise and relate to each other and honour the world around them.

The Yang stream is further elaborated by a colleague of Sharp's, George Lakey.[lxiii] Lakey was part of a movement in the US that spawned two dozen collective houses in Philadelphia during the seventies and eighties as an experiment in "Prefigurative Politics" – attempting to live a post-revolutionary life in the here and now.

Drawing heavily on anarchist theories of organising, Lakey's model includes a phase of "Parallel Institutions" as a way both of undermining the status quo and modelling new more democratic ways of operating. It also seeks to understand and neutralise approaches within the movement that mirror the oppressions of wider society – for example by opposing sexism, racism and homophobia within the movement.

These notions have been absorbed into the Movement of Movements so much that they now seem somehow passé, taken for granted.

What seems to be different in the present moment is that we are moving from a time of limited aims to a time of unlimited dreams. Up until this point our objective has been to resist excess, to topple a dictator, to protest injustice. At some point in the near future these objectives will seem important but insufficient. As the cracks appear in the once impregnable walls of global economic might, we will glimpse the possibility of a new world, shaped by different forces – forces of love, community, care for the soul of the world.

At this point, the prize becomes more compelling than previous aims. It will become human liberation, complete global transformation. The insatiable forces of greed and economic dominance have dragged the world kicking and screaming into a connected interdependent whole. Communications technologies spread aspirations, protests and possibilities with the speed and ferocity of wildfire. Underpinning this is a growing realisation, the awakening of a powerful subconscious longing for a more beautiful, more fulfilling world.

This sense of not settling for second best, this glimpse of a world that allows every child to flourish and flower, will become an unstoppable force – not just in those who have dedicated their lives and souls to change but also in the hearts of many who have hitherto held the levers of power.

This is when we will know the tipping point has been reached – when the political pioneers have won over the sleeping majority and at the same time, enough of the 1% have realised they can let go of an old mode of power and step into a collective process of emergence. This combination of a sustained yearning for change on the streets and crumbling commitment within the citadel of power is what makes a revolution.

8 Minutes of Silence

I once had a conversation with a man I never met again. His name was Martin Kulungu-Banda and he was from Zambia. He had a kind face and hypnotic tales of change on the African continent.

In this conversation, we talk in excited tones about a new method of change, where we forget everything we think we know, because it no longer works. Then we sit, in silence and wait for the future to reveal itself. We sit until she is ready, knowing that she is in charge and will move at her own pace: when she is ready.

Once we are sure we have seen her, we move, following her, doing what we can to clear the undergrowth, call others to follow, pass on what we have seen.

Martin called that moment of waiting 'Presencing'. We wonder, awestruck, what a moment of Global Presencing would look like. How humanity could, together, as a single soul, sit and wait for the future to reveal herself.

Three years later. Nineteen active, conscious individuals from all walks of life, all colours, all ages; nineteen souls who have never met before; come together. We spend the first weekend of 2017 at a small, family-run retreat centre, to consider the state of the world and how to respond to the chaos and turmoil[lxiv]. By the end of the first day we have said all there is to say, shared our vainest hopes and darkest fears. We fall silent. We sit together in spontaneous silence for eight minutes – until the gong sounds for dinner.

As our attention returns to the room, I recall the conversation that birthed the term Global Presencing. What would it look like if the world stopped for a while to allow the future to emerge? What would a truly global process of reimagining civilisation feel like? Someone remarks, "That was it. We just did it."

The following day we compose a collective poem crafted from scraps of words gifted by each person. Lines of truth and tenderness, stitched together:

I hear a call from beyond the soil
in a language I don't understand.
I hear a call to make a choice, make a change.

In a world veiled in the smog of noise
where man is drunk on power
where we feel separate from each other
from nature, from life itself.
In a world of utmost beauty and unbearable terror
a garden spinning in space
filled with infinite possibility
I hear a call
but I choose not to listen.

Life has shown me things I didn't want to see.
Life has shown me what it means to sit at the heart of a wound.
Do not dodge the rocky places or the shadows in the wood.
Learn to inhabit wild space – this is where the magic grows.

In a world of such anger, inequality and complexity
darkness and confusion
ignorance and illusion,
we know how to live the paradox
to lay down fear, cynicism and judgement.
We know how to live in ways that are spacious
Ways that seek silence
We know how to live ways that heal.

I will seek the silence
I will let time flow through me
I will trust I have all I need.

600,000 Souls for Peace

Sharif Abdullah started out as a Black Panther, in the Sixties; a revolutionary advocate of Black Liberation in the US. These were days when the revolution prowled the streets, while its leaders were systematically hunted down, assassinated or imprisoned.

Now Sharif runs an international NGO called Commonway Institute, which is dedicated to "the creation of a society that is in line with our deepest spiritual values – a global society that includes all peoples." During the turning of the millennium, Commonway struck up a long-term partnership with an organisation in war-torn Sri Lanka called Sarvodaya. Here's how they describe what followed:

> *In August of 1999, the Sarvodaya organization started its Peace Initiative, calling for 100,000 people to join in a peace meditation. They got 200,000.*
>
> *The approach is based on the philosophy of inclusivity, a spiritual (but non-religious) knowing that all our lives are inextricably linked, that whatever is done to one is done to all, and that the search for peace has to be based in the notion that all parties to a conflict have to "win".[lxv]*

As the peace movement grew, Sarvodaya organised on-going meditations culminating in the largest the world had seen – over 600,000 people. Peace-makers from around the world were there, including veteran deep-ecologist Joanna Macy (she of the Shambhala Prophecy):

The trains began adding cars, the buses began driving for little or no fee, people started pouring in. What was so moving to me was that you couldn't tell whose side they were on... Physically they had the same brown skin and the same smooth dark hair, and they all wore white.

I remember thinking "all praise be that I have lived to see this moment, that I can experience what it's like for people to come together out of something deeper than their hatred for one another, to come together in their hopes for peace."

There's absolutely no way that I know that you can measure the effectiveness of that. But for those that were there you don't need any external metric...all you know is you've touched some core within yourself that also is the core in everyone else. You've entered a sacred temple that's in each human's heart. (Macy, 2017)

Sharif agrees. In his book **Creating a World that Works for All** he writes:

Do you feel the promise in these perilous times? Despite our many challenges, do these times feel hopeful to you in some way? Does it seem to you that something is ready to change? How are we going to capture the promise that lies within our present predicament?

The hard fact is that getting to a world that works for all will take a more rigorous analysis and more sophisticated actions, both internal and external, than our current political, social, and even spiritual leaders are advocating. It will take fundamental change that must originate with you, as an emerging leader of the new millennium. If our current leadership were capable of it, they would have done it by now.[lxvi]

Sarvodaya is not alone. Since 2011 Mexico has hosted an annual gathering for peace and healing. This has grown from around 12,000 people to over 100,000[lxvii]. David Nicol has studied these types of action and calls them "Subtle Activism" – concrete actions in the world based on the use of subtle energy, meditation and emergence:

To me, the power of subtle activism is simply this: There is nothing we cannot hold in our awareness together. There is no pain, no horror too intense for our collective spiritual presence to bear. Neither is there a level of joy or ecstasy too great for us to expand into with each other.

We are an opening to the infinite, and through us can flow the unlimited powers of the cosmos. And, in being with the reality of our world situation in this way, we perform a service for the whole. Something in us and the world changes for the better.[lxviii]

Nicol's own Gaiafield.net seeks to act as a portal to coordinate such actions, as does Unify.org which has coordinated meditations for global change involving over 100 million people in the course of the past five years.

These mass-meditations are an attempt at Global Presencing. To use Joanna Macy's image, they are designed to connect the core of each to the core of everyone else. It is in this connection that emergence occurs, that the future reveals itself. This is The Field that holds eternal human wisdom, universal wisdom accessible to the human soul. It is The Field beyond all sense of intellect, ego, law, economy, politics. It is pure being and all that is shared by all life: consciousness, love, joy, pain, abundance, connection, grief, beauty. Somewhere amongst all of this is a future waiting to embrace our every hope and expectation.

But to sense into this Field requires a certain degree of openness. Open mind, open heart, open will. We have to be prepared to be shaped by it in unexpected, even uncomfortable ways. We have to first let go of everything we think might be the answer.

Gnawing Away

Then comes the process of using law and rights to stem the onslaught. We can already see what this might look like.

In the space of a week during 2016, three rivers were each granted the full rights of a legal being, a person. "It's always been a living being for us. It's sustained us, spiritually, physically and it's been a food source and every essence of us as a people," says Dianah Ngarogo, a local who runs an adventure business on the Whanganui River in New Zealand.[lxix]

This is both symbolic and real. It is a drop in the ocean of pollution and destruction but a beacon nonetheless. It's a paradigm shift to think of natural phenomena as having equal rights. A paradigm shift for modern times but not so much for our past selves. This is the core of every wisdom tradition, every non-theistic religion, every indigenous culture since time immemorial.

In Ecuador the Constitution not only safeguards:

> *The right of the population to live in a healthy and ecologically balanced environment that guarantees sustainability and the good way of living (sumak kawsay), is recognized.*

But also states:

> *Nature, or Pacha Mama, where life is reproduced and occurs, has the right to integral respect for its existence and for the maintenance and regeneration of its life cycles, structure, functions and evolutionary processes.*

> *All persons, communities, peoples and nations can call upon public authorities to enforce the rights of nature.*

And, interestingly:

> *Nature has the right to be restored. This restoration shall be apart from the obligation of the State and natural persons or legal entities to compensate individuals and communities that depend on affected natural systems.[lxx]*

There are also initiatives such as the international campaign for a Law of Ecocide. Originally initiated by Earth Lawyer, Polly Higgins, this has now become a global movement which attempts to create international law stating the destruction of ecosystems constitutes the crime of ecocide on a par with genocide.[lxxi]

There have been other, smaller successes. A river in New Zealand was granted legal rights following a struggle by the local Maori people:

> *In one of New Zealand's longest running court cases, the iwi won for the river the status of an integrated, living whole, Te Awa Tupua, with rights and interests. Two guardians, one appointed by the iwi and the other by the Crown, will protect those interests.*[lxxii]

Going to Judgement

When Polly Higgins died at the tender age of 50, the church in the picturesque English town of Stroud was packed to the rafters. I have never seen anything like her funeral. There was standing room only. Her brother spoke. And her sister and colleagues. People choked back tears as her husband took to the pulpit.

It was the singer Nick Mulvey who did me in. Playing a hauntingly beautiful rendition of his song *We Are Never Really Apart*, one of Polly's favourites:

> *Nobody said it was simple*
> *But people is it so hard*
> *Knowing who we are*
> *And our place in the stars*
> *And how we*
> *Are never really apart*
> *From the whole of it all.*

Polly described herself as an Earth Lawyer. She'd given up her position as a barrister to defend the Earth and to have the world enact a Law of Ecocide. Her aim was for a global statute that put ecological destruction on a par with genocide.

I learnt a lot from Polly: the value of organic food, the colonial history of sugar, how one person with razor sharp focus can have a global impact. She taught me about tipping points, about bridging the gap to the silent majority and about how the craziness of the modern world was a sign it was nearing its end. She maintained fervently that those who rule the world only do so because we give them the power and permission to do so. People only have power over us for as long as we let them.

And I learnt something about letting go. I took part in Polly's *Dare To Be Great* workshop about eighteen months after my brother died, funnily enough at around the same age as Polly would die five years later. She ran an exercise about letting go of the things that were holding each of us back. I realised that my grief for my brother was getting in the way. I had done it justice, lived with it, made it my friend. I had paid tribute to his life in my grief and paid tribute to my own ability to feel things deeply. Now was the time to let it go. So I did – I screamed and howled at the moon in the depths of the woods, in the depths of night.

There's one more thing that Polly taught me. As I stood amongst the mourners and revellers at her funeral, seeing our shared admiration for someone who had given all she could to her cause, it struck me that we were in danger of making her into an exception. She had dared us all to be great. And it would take that to save the world. Her death was asking us all to step up.

When we do, the transition will slip from the stage of *Gnawing Through* to the stage of *Following*. The course of events will take on its own momentum, less the result of human action, more the flow of the Arc of Time.

A poem for Polly

what have we done
in the rape of our Mother?
Call it what it is.
Breaking into a billion shards
all that is sacred
stars weep molten tears
for our lost way
Then return in a blink to the knowing
this too will pass.
How will we forgive ourselves
in this frenzied age
fracturing the very bond of life giving?
Will a plea of insanity sate the galaxies?
polar ice shatters at the witness of it.
Forests fall
Oceans boil
How did we come to forget ourselves?
these tender sacred selves
here behind this beaten breast bone.
As one more extraordinary soul
steps gently from this teetering edge
laughing softly with the words:
"Over to you now"
We look up to realise
It's over to us
To a billion acts of everyday brilliance
A revolution's worth of ordinary greatness.
It's with us now
Dare we say we've got this?
Say it with me
We've got this, Polly
We've got this.
Say it with me
We've got this.

Inherent in the Times

When I ask people what's regenerative in their life, they invariably smile. It never takes long to answer. Time spent with family and friends. Time in nature, with animals or walking in the woods, by the sea, in the mountains. Creative pursuits, learning to create something of worth and of beauty. And food – growing, gardening, cooking, eating, sharing. For some it might also be something physical – sport, dance, yoga or tai chi. For some it's stillness, quiet, contemplation, reflection.

I have come to understand that whatever is regenerative for Humans is regenerative for the Planet. Whatever is healthy for Humans is healthy for the Planet. And, I theorise, it works in the other direction too: what's right for the Planet is right for People. And what's destructive for the Planet is ultimately (given enough time) destructive for Humankind.

When I say this it seems to make intuitive sense to people. They get that it might be true. When I suggest we should have a Regenerative Movement, that our way of being and working and agitating as The Movement of Movements can only be coherent if everything about it is regenerative, there is a moment of silence. Then a collective "Oh", then we all knuckle down to working out what that means.

Could it be that saving the world might be joyful, full of warmth and creativity? Could it involve looking after ourselves and each other, sharing food, music, dance?

Are these things enough? Does it make a difference if we do them in service to creating a More Beautiful World? Does the addition of conscious action and reflection alchemise these acts into something truly revolutionary? Is it enough to do them or do we need to proclaim that we're doing them?

I'm not sure. Time will tell. The future will let us know. In its own time.

Shake

Gaia is awakening. The dragon-spirit that has slept in the Planet's core for eons is stretching her limbs, unfolding wings from around her drowsy neck. She has been troubled by the clash of metal on sky, shaken from her dreams. Something is out of balance.

Her law is equilibrium in motion. The ebb and flow of predator and prey, the passing of planets, the cycle of time and tide. Without this, one part grows to extreme, moving to excess, consumed by its unbridled shadow.

Gaia shakes the dust from her back, the core of the world shifts, poles realign, ice melts to cool the fever. Wind blows to cleanse air, seas boil against their will, because the air can hold no more heat.

She is moving now, thrice around the circumference of the globe. Scanning landscape for signs of where new life will restore balance. She breathes life in neglected spaces, churning earth and sky, flame and fire.

Nature is healing itself. The gardeners have neglected their task. She will take things back into her own hands. Just for now. Embrace her spirit unconditionally. We cannot know where this leads. Only that there is no other way. Balance will be restored.

Free of Entanglement

Revolution is not what it used to be. It has changed in my lifetime. Perhaps like me it has come of age.

In my adolescent years, when I still knew how to speak truth to power, was full of certainty, could muster righteous indignation from the belly of disdain, revolution was about rage. It was a transformational force of nature that burnt buildings, destroyed the oppressor, uprooted an economic monolith. It had the energy of a wildfire to cleanse and burn and refresh the social soil.

Now it has become the breath of wind on a turning tide. It sighs wistfully: The Revolution is Love, Occupy Your Heart, Give Yourself to Me and I will Make You. It says that even the rich and powerful, the 1%, are not happy within themselves. It asks me to accept that even the oppressor is a prisoner of the system we think they rule over. We are all victims of history, it suggests.

I mouth these words to others, yet I know that embracing them is no easy ask. I thought I had done that work, was able to mean what I say. Until life decided to remind me that these words come with complications, implications. I still have work to do.

Today for instance. I have spent the weekend with a group of young, mostly non-white, urban activists. It has been sometime since I have been in the presence of this amount of pain and wounding.

Every oppression, every agony experienced by the human race, inflicted upon itself, is embodied in these young lives: the day to day violence of racism, the prison of gender – especially for souls that do not fit into binary restrictions. The ravages of war, homelessness, migration, arrival in a cold friendless zone.

I have taught enough people to witness another's pain without absorbing it that I thought I could handle this. I was wrong. On this occasion it was sinking in, hitting home. And when it came time for me to share my own truth I was shaking. I had heard things that made me burn. And at the heart of it all was a way of life designed, built and perpetuated by white men – for the benefit of white men. And that meant me.

159

How could I deny this any longer? How could I think I had accepted it, processed it, and moved on? Was it as simple as setting myself in favour of a new system? Could that really cleanse me? Or a few rituals of grief and atonement? Was any of that enough? Clearly not. If I still felt it, then the work was not yet complete. As long as the system remains in place the hurt is perpetuated.

Yet these young people wanted something different from me. Guilt was certainly no use to them. They understood that even their oppressors are locked into patterns beyond their control. They stopped me getting lost in the self-indulgence of culpability. They needed me to stand alongside them to find a way out, a way forward.

These are people who at a young age feel their lives defined as less worthy due to class, disability, poverty, skin colour. These are lives that have been torn into random strips by childhood sexual exploitation, bullying, street gangs, drugs, mental illness – lives that they are now sticking back together with diligence and care, as they come of age.

A dysfunctional world order, the legacy of slavery and colonisation, the fractures of extreme wealth and mind-perverting power have carved their signatures into the flesh of these lives – in the early death of parents, in the mental health of brothers and sisters, in their own doubts and fears.

In the past I have said I will not carry the guilt for this. In my younger years, while I still had fire, I held the guilt. Maybe it even helped to fuel the fire. I understood the simple truth that it was white men who shaped the system, benefitted from it, ruled over it. I understood it was a zero sum game – some profited at the expense of others.

Then I decided I had atoned enough for this. I had given decades to the struggle against life's multiple intersecting oppressions. I had lived my life as a "New Man", a good father, a caring and loving partner. I had stood in solidarity with the oppressed – marched, protested, boycotted, occupied. And I had participated in ceremony to atone and make good.

But maybe I moved on too quickly. Today I realised that something was still there. I felt the pain of each person as they shared the stories of each wound carefully crafted by life so as to inflict greatest torture.

It was no use to them for me to get stuck in the pain or to reflect it back to them. What they needed was to know their strengths, to be reminded that what had shaped them gave them the energy to change the world, and that to follow that path was both their own salvation and the world's. To know that sitting quiet and still beside their deepest wound was the greatest gift they had to give, the ability to show the world the transformative power of turning suffering into global re-creation.

Bring Fertility Back To Earth

There is another piece to this jigsaw. I feel I may have underplayed it up to now. Was that so I didn't alienate you, the reader? Was it because I was playing it safe? Or is there still some complicity left in these tired bones?

What is it?, you ask. It is to address oppression head on. Have I skirted round it in these pages? And why take this charging bull by the horns at this point?

First and foremost, it is a matter of truth. We did not get here, to this spectacularly prosperous age on equal terms. This really has been a zero-sum game. Some prosper at the expense of others. It is not simply that wealth has been unequally distributed. No. It has been robbed and horded and maintained at the barrel of a gun.

Capitalism is and always has been inseparable from empire, colonialism, exploitation. We have acted, in the West at least, as if it could be cleaned up, as if there was a humane version that was possible. But the historic record says otherwise.

> *"British colonisers set out to transform India into a captive market for British goods. To do that, they had to destroy India's impressive indigenous industries. Before the British arrived, India commanded 27% of the world economy, according to economist Angus Maddison.*
>
> *By the time they left, India's share had been cut to just 3%. The same thing happened to China. After the Opium Wars, when Britain invaded China and forced open its borders to British goods on unequal terms, China's share of the world economy dwindled from 35% to an all-time low of 7%.*
>
> *Meanwhile, Europeans increased their share of global GDP from 20% to 60% during the colonial period. Europe didn't develop the colonies. The colonies developed Europe."*[lxxiii]

One estimate suggests that Britain alone benefited to the tune of £6.5 trillion, yes trillion, just from the slave trade[lxxiv]. This at the expense of the 12 million people enslaved in the Americas, plus countless others who died at sea. It is hard to fathom the real implications of either this financial gain or the human toll. Its ripples continue to touch lives in all three continents that were part of this dark and tragic trade.

So the first task is to bear witness to what has gone before. To not brush it under the carpet. The second task is to recognise that the intricate fabric of racism, patriarchy, prejudice, empire, will have to be carefully unpicked stitch by stitch – in our minds, in our schools, our books, our language, our body language even.

Perhaps we will need some atonement, some recognition, even some reparation. Certainly there is ample space and abundant need for healing. These traumas run so very deep. They will not easily be healed overnight.

And there are two other reasons for looking this daemon in the eye. Firstly, if this revolution is to be different, if it is to avoid the mistakes of the past, to end the repeating cycle of history, it must be the revolution of the entire human species. It must restore the order of one family on equal terms, without the slightest hint of power by one section over another.

And secondly, there is a secret that the most oppressed, exploited and marginalised have been guarding for the past five centuries. A line of knowledge and wisdom they have faithfully protected against the onslaught of colonisation, white supremacy and patriarchy. I'll let John Liu tell it how it is:

> We need to consider the fact that many peoples who are now "poor" are often descendant from cultures that were brutally abused and suppressed by the ancestors of those who are now wealthy. This is not because it is advisable to seek to blame or retaliate for ancient crimes but to promote truth and reconciliation and to close that chapter in history. We need to honor the knowledge these cultures had and that was ignored as the colonizing powers choose to spread materialistic market economics that has led humanity to mass desertification, biodiversity loss and climate change.
>
> When we recognize that the cultures that were conquered were actually higher civilizations than the conquerors we also have

163

to realize that the reason they were superior is that they protected their landscapes in ecologically functional ways that did not lead to the calamities that are now befalling us. This recognition reveals a truth that has been forgotten. Namely, that ecological function is more valuable that things.

If we put this concept at the center of our thinking now we can move from a materialist economy to an ecological economy. This has numerous benefits. We can correct historical mistakes. We can evolve human consciousness. We can shift from a corrupt and destructive economy of consumption to a fair and abundant economy based on ecological health benefiting all living things and ensuring a safe future for generations to come.[lxxv]

Privilege

I cannot know what my ancestors did.
As they crossed the prairie of Kansas
did they massacre Indians?
or turn a blind eye as others did?
Or maybe they were sickened by it and kept moving West.
Did they shoot Indians in the Black Hole of Kolkata?
Trade slaves from Gorée Island to Recife, Kingston or
Alabama?
Maybe they fought a war to sell opium to the Chinese
Empire
Or to conquer Zimbabwe, Sudan and 67 other lands.
I cannot know these things.
What I know is
this nation was built on all this.
These streets run red with the world's blood.
The taint of it soils my food, the tea, the sugar, the spices
It stains the clothes on my back, the sheets on this bed.
What I know is
the stench of it chokes the currents of the air.
For in the doing of it all
we cut down the lungs of the world
ripped people from the land they had nurtured for an age
poisoned rivers that once ran pure.
And in the doing of it all
set in train the chain of events that now threatens our
extinction.
Yes.
Look into the horror of it.
This climate emergency is the fruit of Empire
And the source of my privilege.
What I know is
this must stop now.
We can bear it no longer.

Empire must fall
Patriarchy must die.
What I know is
reparation must be made
Museums emptied of their loot
Artefacts returned to the sacred sites they were fashioned to
protect
Balance restored to the sacred geometry
of this sweet Earth.
What I know is
this ends here.
Or we will pay with our lives
And the lives of our ancestors to come.

8. The Light Endures

How Should we Approach this Time of Transition?

This is a time to continue on, to endure on your path and in what is right. Be constant, regular and stable. Have a definite direction or plan and follow it constantly. Cling to established principles now.

As you complete one thing, let it become the start of the next. The sun and moon depend on heaven, thus their light endures.

The wise person endures in this way, thus the human world can change and perfect itself. If you contemplate where and how things persevere, you will see the deep purpose of all the myriad beings.

[I Ching 32. Persevering]

Constant, Regular and Stable

What is to be done? To continue on. To have a plan and be constant.

What does this mean? If the spirit of revolution, revolutionary love, had a voice what might it say?

> *Don't panic. We have boundless amounts of time. The universe is constant, gracefully arcing time. What feels urgent now is a blink in the eye of the cosmos. You can afford to take your time.*

> *The Earth is not in peril. For sure, Humankind will undergo turbulent change but isn't that what you want? You will survive if you evolve. Evolution is the driving force of the Universe. It means to adapt and respond to change. To move purposefully towards abundance, to refine consciousness so that it sees how things grows, thrive and persist in a state of dynamic equilibrium.*

> *Your dark side has always had a morbid fascination with Armageddon. Let go of the drama for a while. It's not doing you any good. It's not doing the planet any good.*

> *Sure, there will be change and yes, it's likely to get pretty hairy. There will be more suffering in the transition that there might have been. But there is nothing you can do about that. That is just the shadow of man (yes, man) working its way out. Sad as that might be, that's the way it has to be. You have to get through this shadow in order to reach the light - the place of what's possible for humankind.*

There is nothing to be done. The revolution will not be won. We will wake up one day to find the world has changed and we hadn't even noticed.

There is nothing to be done but persisting. Just keep going. Use small, practised, careful steps to continue on our path.

The system will not be overthrown. It will be overgrown. A new world will one day swallow up the dying remnants of empire. It will become irresistible, obvious. Why didn't we do this earlier? Why didn't we all simply step into the flow?

The Arc of Time has one shape. It bends in one direction. It has a gravitational pull that can be resisted but never overcome.

What is the Established Principle, the Direction that is Right? As with the individual, it is the same with us all, as a whole. Once we become aware of our truest purpose there is nothing we can do but follow it. At first it pulls us, nudges, cajoles. Then it is simply a matter of stepping into it, drifting along on the current.

We must find our truest purpose and persist with it. When things are stretched to breaking point, we must persist. When one thing is finished we move on to the next. Once we have this true direction, there is nothing to do but follow it.

Every year the Oasis School of Human Relations, where I carry out my work, holds a gathering. We call together our wider community of practitioners to explore how the world is changing and how we want to respond. It is a nourishing time where relationships are strengthened and renewed, where ideas are aired and plans fermented.

During one of these gatherings I took a walk with two of my colleagues. We must have looked an odd group walking through the backstreets of the small Yorkshire town of Boston Spa – me a middle-aged white guy eager and earnest, Tahmina a bubbly South Asian woman half my age and full of passion and energy, Irwin a lumbering Caribbean man with a deep voice, a wicked smile and an incurably inquisitive nature.

The sun was shining, the air was clean and fresh and the conversation flowed in the way it does when souls meet. We were talking about the things that get under our skin – Tahmina the destruction of the oceans, Irwin the way we just can't live together, me, actually I can't remember what.

Then the conversation turned to how to get out of the mire we felt stuck in. We decided that eco-systems operate in some form of dynamic harmony when each thing is playing its own distinct role as part of the whole – and the harmony disappears if any one element gets out of control, unchecked by the equilibrium of the others. Imbalance comes from domination. Balance from purpose.

I mentioned a book I had recently read which ended on the question, "What if humanity as a species had a purpose?" What is the one distinct contribution that we give to the whole? Having circled the village we stopped in the road leading back to Oasis. The weight of the question required a pause.

"I think I've found the answer," I ventured. "Whenever I dwell on this question, one word just kept coming back: abundance. Our species-purpose is to bring abundance to the entire system. We are able to consciously tend to all things so they can all thrive."

"It's like we're the Gardeners," Irwin offered.

"Yes. That's it. We're the Gardeners. If we weren't here the jungle would return. Instead, we can bring creative equilibrium to the system. We have mistaken our purpose for thinking we could just take whatever we want from the garden because we have dominion over it. When really our job is to tend it all."

Mundane as it is, beneath us as it may seem, our purpose on this Earth is simply to tend this breath-taking, beautiful, abundant, ever-shifting world of ours. We are destined to be its stewards, designed by the evolutionary pulse of the Universe to consciously, meticulously tend its every corner until life in all its infinite glory returns to maturity. Then we get to sit back and enjoy the infinite wonder of it all.

Life as Sex

Life could be like sex. The best sex you've ever had. It could be about surrender, trust, following the path of pleasure, giving and receiving, moving in response to the flow, following your own needs while serving another. And all the while blissfully oblivious to the passage of time, completely absorbed in the moment.

Even saying this in our day and age is problematic. There is so much guilt and shame tied up in sex. So much violence, exploitation and anger imprinted upon it by abuse, harassment, the constant aggression that underlies forcing seven billion sexual beings into two sexual roles and a whole plethora of regulations to police them.

This is no coincidence. The simple key to the more beautiful future is for each of us to follow our calling with all the joy and passion our heart can muster. And to do so, not for selfishness or hedonism, but in service of all life on this Earth.

Sexual violence is all about power. This much is plain. But power can be exerted in many different ways – violence, manipulation, intimidation. So why sex? Could it be that the best way to mess with someone, to really mess with their body and soul, is to mess with the primal life-force that shapes, feeds and directs them. Break that and you break them, for a while at least.

The best way to try to control the future is to screw over our present sexuality. Our calling is fed by our sexual energy. It is our fuel. When we sit squarely in a grounded, powerful sexuality we are in our prime, in control, as able as ever to cope with whatever life throws at us. We are in touch with our purpose, our personal power, our authentic being. Pervert the power that feeds this and it can become difficult to know what we are really about.

That's why ending sexual violence and repairing the damage of trauma are central to restoring the balance of life. That's why anything that breaks the tyranny of binary gender roles and the violence of patriarchal sex will help liberate humanity and awaken it to its fullest potential.

Sexual Energy

Sexual energy is the magnetism that creates the pull back to oneness... It is inherent within life, the primal force that drives evolution, procreation, proliferation and expansion. This interconnects all of us, it's the driving force of humanity...

The misunderstanding is that when you feel it arise in your body, it is to be acted out. Actually, it's just the pulsating vibration that is coursing through your life and through your trajectory... It's a breathing, moving pulsing essence in your life...

It's good to get in touch with that primal force. It's good to get in touch with your own sexuality, with your own relationship, with feeling infused with this force of life and knowing where that drive, that dynamism is taking you. Then you can compare whether a person or an environment or a decision is in alignment with that driving force...

If you want to distort the collective, you go to the primal source that moves everything. It's like poisoning the main source of the water; then it goes throughout the entire system. If the primal essence of the collective is sexual energy, where does the deepest distortion go if you want control over people? It's what we do in relationships too – make people feel guilt or shame to control them.

So the cleansing of this is to be in integrity, to hold yourself in alignment with your own sexual energy... Then there's less distortion. There's less need to manipulate, or to get something from someone else.

Jocelyn Daher, writer and Life Coach[lxxvi]

Liquid Gold

I fell in love with life today.

It may have been the achingly beautiful soul walking with me. Or the crisp winter sun picking out perfect walled squares on the side of the dale. Or the way no pain we held was too raw to touch. It may have been many things, all these things. Who am I to say.

Letting go of the bank, I slipped softly into the stream.

"I don't think I can let go," I murmured.

She said, "That feeling probably means you already have."

"I'd like to think so," I replied, "but maybe that's just delusion."

"It's all delusion." She laughed softly. "Just pick the one you want."

We strode up to the edge of the abyss where sun caressed the belly of the hills below, soft as the back of her hand, sharp as a knife to my eye. Beer-brave nearly-men dangled themselves from a tree to look out over the edge.

Unable to watch, we walked and talked instead of how the pain in men was destroying them and destroying the world. We walked and talked of the impossibility of saving the planet and of how it would be done. And whether any of us would survive to tell the tale.

We witnessed each other's pain – the one that gnaws away at the bottom of our gut, occupying the space where love is meant to live. Letting go of the urge to help, I watched her cry until she came up for air. Then I took the rock and holding it tight to my chest, sank to the bottom where the stain in my family's past was indistinguishable from the murkiness that has corrupted the world.

When we resurfaced, we told the stories we tell about ourselves. "Put each one down," she advised. "Put each one down until you can see your truer self... I don't believe there is a truer self, but this is how you find it."

"There are two stories I tell about myself," I ventured. "One is: I don't get enough love."

She said, "The thing to let go of is not even that. It is that love is a thing to get. It is all around. Everything is made of it. The Universe is love. You are love. Pure liquid gold. Within and without."

173

I closed my eyes to let the words sink in but somehow couldn't quite get my head around it. So I took her hands across the table. "Ah. Yes. You're right. I feel it now."

"What's the second story?"

"It's already gone."

"Good," she smiled. "You're getting the hang of this."

Outside the stars crept across the sky, dusting the cars with frost and calling us out into the fragile air. Falling into the stream again, we gave ourselves up to the unbearable beauty of the ether painted out above our heads. "Fuck! This is gorgeous. Life is a joy, a gift."

This is how you fall in love, you see. When the pain and grace of it all is just too much to hold any longer. So you give in and let yourself be swept up in the beauty of every cell caught in every shaft of light and every breath of frost on every blade of grass and every first glint in the eye of a kindred spirit. Well at any rate, that's how I fell in love today.

Lions

Remember: we are many. Just because we are a cave full of slumbering lions does not mean we will never wake. We woke before and we shall wake again to defend what's sacred.

Even while we rest we do so in honour of Earth. We sleep-plant, sleep-reforest, sleep-recycle, sleep-heal ...

When all sleep-walking is done we shall dance wildly reclaiming, rejoicing, remembering, regenerating, revolting. Roaring rebels with a cause. That cause is Home. Our earth.

Clio Pauly, Namibia

Letter from the Seventh Generation

This week we're writing to our ancestors. The Elders thought it would be a good thing to do. Some of my friends are angry at you because of what you did. The Elders thought writing you a message would help.

I'm not angry. I know you did what you could. You were trapped inside a story that you were born into. It was a time that was out of control and caused all kinds of things that no-one really wanted. I know no-one really wants to destroy the life all around them, to dirty the land and water and seas. That's just stupid.

Some of my friends are real angry, so angry it makes them sad. They say you nearly destroyed the planet. That we nearly weren't here because of you. They say you killed off lions and monkeys and frogs and birds and fishes.

My brother says you did all this to get money to fill your homes with stuff because your lives were empty. My friends say they can hear the ghosts of all the dead creatures howling at night. They see the rivers running red with blood or black with tar. They say even the mountains cry and grieve. Some of my friends say you nearly killed the whole human race by changing the weather so the seas died and the crops wouldn't grow and the air was too dirty to breathe.

I guess this may be true but you can look at it the other way too. You actually saved the planet when it was most in danger. Some of our people say your souls chose to be alive in the time of chaos. If it's true then I think you were really brave. I think it wasn't easy to be born in a time when we nearly destroyed ourselves. When everyone was at war with each other and with different parts of their soul.

This sounds very scary to me. Was it scary? Was it terrible with all the pollution and everything dying all around you? Did you need to lock your heart in a box so it didn't break into pieces like the glass I dropped when I was washing up last week?

We say don't judge me before you've walked in my shoes. So I try to think what your reason was. Why some of you were so selfish or angry and ruined things. The Elders say what sits under all destruction is pain – like a wounded animal, cornered and scared. So I think some of your people were sad and hurt and hadn't gotten the grief and pain out of their blood so it made them a bit crazed and selfish and not thinking right.

Anyway, I'm not angry. I want to say thank you. Thank you for choosing to be alive and to do what you could. Thank you for being calm and not making things worse. That would have been the end of everything.

And especially thank you for doing all those wiz things to start planting the seeds of our life. Thank you for rediscovering earth regen practices, for paying attention to the movement of spirit. I love you for this. And I love you for having babies. Because otherwise I wouldn't be here. And I love being here now. This has to be the best time ever.

Thank you. I love you. I hope my friends will love you too. I think they will if they say enough forgiveness prayers. You may know it. It goes like this "I see how it has been. I'm sorry it was like this for you. Please forgive me. I love you. Thank you."[lxxvii]

Marina, in her ninth year.

Cling to Established Principles

In times of transition the existing order weakens. Small acts cast waves beyond their usual magnitude. Especially acts that model the capacity for a new world. The possibilities are constrained only by the creativity of human imagination.

That time is now. It is no longer enough to mouth words, to teach, implore, philosophise. Now is the time to be the change. Clinging to established principles means to live, embody, enact our values in every detail of the day-to-day. There is beauty in the simple. There is regeneration in tending to others, to the land, to the call of your very soul.

So what next for me? I don't plan leaving this, my last life, before I have reached my own intrinsic limits. There is more to come. I am a little over halfway there.

The way forward is clear if I follow the path that can be traced from the point of my death back to this present. I have seen my own death. Not the moment itself, but the circumstances around it, its nature.

As I sat and watched my eldest brother die on a hospital bed, a little after his fiftieth birthday, death taught me that it is the culmination of a life. It is the point at which everything that is possible in that life comes to fruition. At this point all potential, all possibility is achieved and death moves in to end the flow and make space for something else. Death is the resolution of life – its gifts, its flaws, its idiosyncrasies.

So I have envisioned my own death. It comes at the point that I embrace trust and love to such an extent that I can let go of life. It comes at the point that I am at peace with everything about my life, myself, the world around me. This peace is what allows me to let go of living. And I return home, to the endless swirl of energy that fills the space between heaven and earth.

Tracing back from that point means for me to live a life that embodies everything I know to be true. It means narrowing the gap between word and deed. It means living the New Story.

When I took up the I Ching I decided to live in accordance with the Readings it offered me. If I believed they were echoes of the future finding their way to my desk then I could trust in their guidance, even if they went against my world view, my beliefs or what my ego wanted me to do.

When they told me not to act, I sat on my hands, however hard that was. When they told me to find emptiness, I watched my bank account empty and tried not to panic. When they told me to grasp the opportunity, I lunged at life with passion and joy.

The Readings about our fate talk of small things, drudgery, living close to the Earth, bringing forth the feminine. This is my life now. To live this life in each and every moment. To show it is possible, to show it can be joyful, to show it can regenerate the Planet.

The revolution cannot be shaped alone. It is a collective endeavour wrought by friends and neighbours, unexpected allies working for a more beautiful life together. It arrives in the moment everyone becomes an activist because everyone is consciously co-creating their dream future, not as isolated selfish individuals, but as a collective whole.

Endure on The Path

The I Ching has thwarted me at every turn. My study of political science told me social change happens through the revolutionary overthrow of one order by another. The I Ching said we are going through a transformation and that there is nothing to be done.

Social sciences told me power must be wrenched from the hands of the powerful against their will. The I Ching said act through the feminine, do not impose your will. Socialism told me a bright new future of egalitarianism would follow the death of capitalism. The I Ching said endure the crisis that follows collapse.

Science and technology told me human ingenuity would save us with green technologies, the internet of things and artificial intelligence. The I Ching said hide your brightness and follow the path of drudgery that's beneath you.

Everything I thought I knew, everything that seemed certain was overturned. Dreams of a utopian future of wealth, progress and comfort were replaced by collapse, regrowth and the dignity of manual labour. The more I tried to keep hold of a vision of human society triumphing over adversity, the more the I Ching insisted the answer was small things, allowance, perseverance. There was no grand vision or masterplan. Only enduring principles stretched to their limit: return to balance in nature.

Eventually I succumbed. I realised there was a simple logic in it. To heal the world means to care for it. To dedicate our time and effort to this and this alone. And to do it through the Yin: the energy of quiet allowance, the archetypal feminine power of nurturing, caring, birthing. Everything else was ego, hubris, pride, a vain attempt at imposing will, rather than going with the eternal flow.

Once I accepted this, I soon got a little bored. Bored of hearing myself say and write these words. It didn't feel at all satisfying to talk about regenerating the planet or to be slightly in awe of those who were doing it. If it was that important, I had to learn to do it too – not just talk about it.

I took a permaculture course. My wife Sheila, the woman who has shared my life, from childhood to these mid-afternoon years, came too.

It was hosted at an eco-village in Ireland. We loved what it promised so much we decided to take a year exploring similar communities to see what they had to offer.

Within seven months we'd sold our house and moved into an intentional community based in a 40 acre organic farm. This is where we live now, slowly finding our place in the rhythm of the seasons, finding our place amongst the 50 people, aged from 1 to 71 who tend the land, prune the trees, milk the cows and plant the garden.

There is a lifetime of things to learn and explore: the balance between beauty and functionality, between abundance and sufficiency, personal space and community. Some of this learning is already known, some is new to us but not others. Some will be very specific to this place, to the climate, the soil, the heritage of plants and crops, the mix of people involved. Much will be transferable at the level of principle to anywhere in the world.

There are laws at work, laws of human life, nature, the machinations of the cosmos itself. Gradually we are learning these and what they mean for the way we live the rest of our lives. Little is absolute, much is trial and error, learning for the sake of experimentation.

This, for me at least, is the learning the world needs most right now. How to produce the things we need from the belly of the earth? How to replenish the land both for us and for all life that inhabits it? How to acknowledge the mistakes of the past and put them right for the future? And how to live together with others in shared endeavour, not sweeping anything under the carpet, but neither turning a drama into a crisis?

And all the while, learning the art of change and perfection. Learning how to refine a human life by integrating it into the fabric of the land, the air, the water, sky and forests that cradle it. How to accept the movements of the cosmos and live a life rocked by their ebb and flow. How to respect the Laws of Nature, the Laws of Spirit, the Laws of the Universe, seeing them as taking precedence over the Laws of Humankind.

Time is on our side. My heart sees us all in our autumn years sitting together soaking up the sun between the vegetable patches and the fruit trees, playing with our grand-children – or someone else's. We have all the time we need.

dedication

My life is no longer my own.
I have marked my face
with red earth and white clay
pricked out the seven centres of being
with blood from this left hand.

I have walked the circle
bare foot and bare chest
in full view of Long Meg and Her Daughters
casting shards from Old Oraibi
before climbing the back of Pendragon's stone
all the while
giving over what remains of these days
in service to beauty
possibility
fearless avowal -
all the while
dedicating myself
to dissolving this soul
into the fertile dance
of love, connection, convocation.

My life is no longer my own
was never mine to own
belonged always
to the subtle force
shifting stars
in the unseen sky.

My life belongs to revolution
devotion
reunion.

Letter to the Seventh Generation

Dear Marina,

Thank you for your kind letter. Your words carry the wisdom of an Elder and the purity of youth.

You cannot know how wonderful it is to realise that you are there, alive, enjoying the best time ever. There are moments now when I think we will not make it. Sad moments when I think we will destroy everything and no-one will be able to survive.

Sometimes this makes me angry – like some of your friends. Sometimes I want to scream because I have no idea what to do that will make any of it stop.

But mostly I feel sad. Sad because we are a beautiful, creative, clever species. We are able to see the divinity in everything, to make beautiful music, paint wonderful watercolours. We have the chance to live a life beyond our wildest dreams. Then I get sad at the thought that we are in danger of throwing it all away.

Knowing that you are there, that we made it through, that you have made something from the ashes we left you, that makes me very, very happy.

Your friends have a right to be angry. What we are doing now is like a madness. I can't explain it. There are times when nothing makes sense to me. We have just forgotten how to live in harmony with the world around us. Maybe you are right – we are hurt, our lives are empty, we have moved too far from the wisdom of nature.

The reason behind this madness doesn't matter. What matters is that somewhere along the line, our sons and grand-daughters and their children found a way to heal the wounds and to start again. I hope and trust that the way I am living my life is part of this process.

I know there have been some difficult times between my world and yours. I know that the generations between us have been through much hardship and hard work. And I know that this will be worth it in the end.

I thank you and them for all you have done for us. I want to say something back to you, to your mother and father, their parents and all the generations between us:

I see how it has been for you.
I'm sorry it has been like this.
Please forgive me.
I love you.
Thank you.

The Map of a Miracle

The Catastrophe Story carries so much weight because our collective memory recognises it well. This is the same story that has arisen again and again since biblical times. Our myths and legends are full of it – empires rising and falling, collapsing in catastrophic fashion. Sometimes it is a natural disaster, like Pompeii. More often it is the corruption and decadence of the society itself – or those who rule it, that brings things crashing down.

This pattern has seeped into our DNA. Our bodies carry a warning alarm when we feel it approaching. For some of us this is a subtle unease. For others a much stronger sense of foreboding. This is what The Movement of Movements has tapped into. We feel collapse approaching with almost inevitable momentum.

Whether it's the fall of the first cities of the Fertile Crescent or the Roman Empire, the end of the Mayan civilisation, Greater Zimbabwe, Benin, Easter Island, Chaco Canyon, or the rhythmic shifts of Chinese Dynasties, somewhere in our ancestral past we have experienced this before.

And so we pass through the well-trodden phases of denial, anger, bargaining and desolation before eventually deciding whether or not there is anything we can do to rewrite history this time round. Or deciding that even if there isn't, we're going to try anyway.

Then two other archetypal stories start to weave their threads. The first, George Monbiot has called the Restoration Story. He describes it like this:

> *Disorder afflicts the land, caused by powerful and nefarious forces working against the interests of humanity. But the hero will revolt against this disorder, fight those powerful forces, against the odds overthrow them and restore harmony to the land.*
>
> *You've heard this story before. It's the Bible story. It's the "Harry Potter" story. It's the "Lord of the Rings" story. It's the "Narnia" story. But it's also the story that has accompanied almost every political and religious transformation going back millennia.*

In fact, we could go as far as to say that without a powerful new restoration story, a political and religious transformation might not be able to happen. It's that important.lxxviii

This too is a story so universal it lives within our DNA. David and Goliath: the righting of wrongs against all odds.

Then the third story starts to whisper in the firelight. It is the story of humanity's ability to overcome seemingly insurmountable odds, told by the breeze playing songs in the branches of Poplar Trees. Tall, graceful sentries of the land. Their symbolism in ancient British folklore is of abundance, divination, resilience: the ability of humanity to overcome even the most intractable problems.

They remind us that when our lives are thrown into chaos we are able to muster inner strength we didn't know we had. And we are called to band together with those around us to give selflessly so that the collective can survive – even if we personally do not.

This Survival Story, The Story of Transcendence, has been recounted by Rebecca Solnit in her study of how communities respond to disasters.lxxix She says:

> *Disaster… drags us into emergencies that require we act, and act altruistically, bravely and with initiative in order to survive or save your neighbors.*

She continues:

> *In the wake of an earthquake, a bombing, or a major storm, most people are altruistic, gently engaged in caring for themselves and those around them, strangers and neighbours as well as friends and loved ones. The image of the selfish, panicky or regressively savage human being has little truth in it. Decades of meticulous sociological research… have demonstrated this.*

A crisis really can bring out the best in human nature. This collective awakening and empowerment creates the miracle needed to transcend a catastrophe.

There's another dynamic that Rebecca Solnit also identifies. It is that it's the people, acting outside the normal structures that creates this transcendence. Formal systems often act aggressively and/or repressively, fearing disorder and chaos. The people on the other hand, band together to support each other, even if they are strangers and even if this seems against their own personal best interests. It brings out a kind of revolutionary solidarity:

> *If paradise now arises in hell, it's because in the suspension of the usual order and the failure of most systems, we are free to live and act another way.*

These three stories, Catastrophe, Restoration, Transcendence, burnt into our DNA through the repetition of history, will guide us through the transformation to come. With each of them are archetypes that we intuitively recognise, too. As we sense the approach of catastrophe we begin to see at our feet archetypal paths emerging from the undergrowth. Paths trodden many times by our ancestors, in myths, in legends, in days of old.

There's the path of **Speaking Truth to Power**. This was the path of Jonah in the Old Testament. You remember, he was swallowed by the whale. This happened because Jonah was trying to avoid going into the lion's den (to mix my biblical metaphors) to confront the corrupt leaders of his time. Eventually, after being spewed up by the whale he relented and travelled to Nineveh where he was able to convince the corrupt of the error of their ways and turn the city around (at least for a while).[lxxx]

The second is the path of the **Shambhala Warrior**, the Tibetan legend which describes how at a time when the world is in peril, peaceful warriors go into the corridors of power and dismantle them brick by brick. One step on from Speaking Truth to Power, this is the active, careful and compassionate deconstruction of the systems and institutions of unequal power which are destroying the world.

Both of these paths invite us to confront the structures of power head on. The third path is different. It is to **Head for the Hills**. These folk have given up on civilisation as it is, recognising that all is lost. Like Moses leading the Jews out of Egypt, we head from the heart of darkness towards the promised land. And when we find safety we create what anarchists call an Autonomous Zone where we can establish a new civilisation.

Is there a choice to be made between these approaches? Is one more effective, more timely, more successful than another? I can't be sure. It strikes me that at this point it is impossible to say which approach is most called for. Times are too uncertain, too fluid.

Why not prepare for all three? We could try them together. Or in sequence. If we do nothing else, let's each take a step onto one or other path, knowing we can move easily between them. Choose whichever suits you best in this moment. As long as we remain conscious of what we're doing and stay awake to whether or not it's working, what is there to lose?

And there can be a balance between them. I like what Pancho Ramos Stierle said during the Occupy era: *"I believe that nine out of ten actions must be creating the community that we want to live in"*. The tenth can be an act of resistance or truth-telling. Personally, that's about all my energy levels can take. I find far more joy and excitement and community in creating the new than in battling the old.

With these three stories and these three archetypes we start to build the map we need to get us through the coming turmoil. I hope in these pages I have helped to sketch out other parts of the map – the destination that awaits us if we follow the healthy, loving and generous aspects of our inner nature.

Rebecca Solnit quotes Oscar Wilde in her book:

> *A map of the world that does not include Utopia is not worth even glancing at, for it leaves out the one country at which humanity is always heading.*

All of this really is coded into our bodies. The Map to Utopia is the map of the human heart. But of course, as we know only too well, there is a shadow side to us too. Perhaps surprisingly, Solnit observes that this is only very rarely evident amongst those living through a catastrophe. While the media might focus on indiscriminate looting or desperate behaviour, this is far less common than you'd expect. More often than not, a disaster brings out the best in folk – generosity, community, purpose. It create everyday miracles where each and every one of us do things we never imagined we were capable of.

No, if the shadow arises, it is not in the hearts of those in the thick of the crisis. Motivated by fear, stoked by rumour and misinformation, it arises in a frantic attempt by those insulated by power, to establish control over the situation. She dubs this "Elite Panic". Sometimes emanating from self-interest or self-preservation, other times motivated by the maintenance of order and control. It is the bearing down by the powerful and it creates suffering and injury.

Paradoxically, studies have demonstrated that command and control is near useless in a crisis. It is too slow, too centralised, too unresponsive. Only decentralised self-management can do what's needed on the ground.

So it will be for us, for the world, as we move further into the Global Transformation. The future is not yet written, even if the Arc bends inexorably towards justice and right. As we sit here today there is still the possibility that as a species we will not make it. There is also the possibility that repression and authoritarian populism will win out.

Avoiding either of these outcomes will depend on our collective ability to take a deep breath, steady our nerve and trust that together we have all we need. It is that state of intrinsic calm that gets people out of a burning building without trampling over each other. An almost out-of-body state, where time stands still, then moves at half the normal speed and we are guided by who-knows-what. This is the state that runs through the Seven Mantras. It is the state we will need to embody day-in, day-out over coming years.

Our situation may also take a miracle. Luckily, as we've seen, miracles are what we're made of – especially in an emergency. Navigating that emergency will take everything we've got – and a bunch of stuff we don't even know we are capable of. Survival will also depend on avoiding the backlash, violence and chaos of an Elite Panic.

As we head now into the days that will determine the future of humanity, our very survival, we will need to keep our eyes firmly on the prize, using every fibre of mind, body and soul to create the More Beautiful World Our Hearts Know Is Possible. And out of the corner of our eye, we will do well to stay attuned to the need to not spook the elites who have brought us to the brink of disaster. This will require every ounce of generosity, forgiveness and calm we can muster. If we're lucky that in itself will be the very making of us.

Acknowledgements

There are a wealth of people, processes, resources and moments in time that have supported the creation of this work. It feels an impossible task to acknowledge them all and to do them justice. Perhaps you were part of this. Or perhaps you will be part of its onward transmission. If so, thank you. You know the part you played.

Perhaps I should start with my ancestors, my family, my wife and children, all of whom have shaped me and allowed the writing to come forward. Then there are the friends, colleagues at Oasis and now the community that stands around me, without which I would not be able to write and work and be.

There are three processes that stand out as opening doorways to ways of being and knowing that allowed this work to come to life. First was a conference of Native American and Maya elders, held in Albuquerque in 2012. This was my first embodied introduction to the indigenous world view. Second was The New Story Summit at Findhorn in 2014, where I met many of the people who appear in these pages. Third has been my involvement with the Band of Brothers community in the UK. Here I found rage and grief, companionship and came to own, love and honour a grounded, beautiful form of masculinity.

I am now deeply embedded within Extinction Rebellion which has become the tribe of which I'm a member. Soul mates and fellow travellers in the Movement of Movements.

When it comes to the writing, I must thanks Alison Davies for her support in the earliest iterations, Rose Drew and Gil Coombes for the final version. Thank you for believing in this work.

And lastly, a huge thank you to everyone whose words, Facebook posts and poetry have found their way into these pages. I have tried to do you justice, tried to use my position of privilege to put forward your voices. I trust I have represented the spirit of your work.

Photo Credits

Some of the photos included have been taken from Facebook or from an individual's internet presence. Not all of these photos were credited or can be traced. I have done my best to credit those that I can. This has been done in good faith. If I have missed your credit, I sincerely apologise. Please let us know and we will put it right as and when we can.

All photos have been modified and rendered to black and white by the author.

Chapter Dividers by Laura Cadman.

The milky way – credit unknown
Rhonda Fabian – Facebook
Joanna Macy – uncredited
Lyla June – Tony Calek, from Facebook
Cynthia Jurs – Facebook
Buffalo – Laurenz Stoisser
Rainbow – the author
Vandana Shiva – Vandana Shiva Images
Woman Stands Shining – Facebook
Thich Nhat Hahn – uncredited
Sit Down, Rise Up – Flickr, David Shackbone
Pancho Ramos Stierle – uncredited phot from Upaya.org
Candles in Sri Lanka – unknown
Clio Pauly – Facebook

Resources

Books

The following books have influenced the concepts, thoughts and feelings in these pages. I am equally indebted to all the people whose Facebook posts and YouTube videos have contributed to this work.

Abdullah, Sharriff, Creating a World That Works for All, Berrett-Kohler Publishers 1999

Bardi, Ugo, The Limits to Growth Revisited, Springer, 2011

Brock, Adam, Change Here Now, North Atlantic Books, 2017

Bucko, Adam, Occupy Spirituality, North Atlantic Books, 2013

Buddha, The Teachings of Buddha, compiled by Paul Carus, Rider, 1915

Diamond, Jared, Collapse: How Societies Choose to Fail or Succeed, Penguin, 2011

Eisenstein, Charles, The More Beautiful World Our Hearts Know Is Possible, North Atlantic Books, 2013

Eisenstein, Charles, Climate – A New Story, North Atlantic Books, 2018

Engler, Mark & Paul, This is an Uprising, Bold Type Books, 2016

Estes, Clarissa Pinkola, Women Who Run With the Wolves, Ballantine Books, 1992

Extinction Rebellion, This Is Not a Drill, Penguin, 2019

Forest, Ohky Simine, Dreaming the Council Ways, Samuel Weiser, 2000

Gladwell, Malcolm, The Tipping Point, Back Bay Books, 2000

Hawken, Paul, Blessed Unrest, Penguin, 2007

Huai-Chin Nan, Tao and Longevity, Element Books, 1988

Kosha, Joubert & Leila Dregger (eds), Ecovillages, 1001 ways to heal the planet, Triarchy Press, 2015

Karcher, Stephen, How to Use the I Ching, Element Books, 1997

Lakey, George, Towards a Living Revolution, Peace News Press, 2012

Lao Tzu, Tao Te Ching, ed. Ursula K Le Guin, Shambhala Publications, 1998

Levine, Peter, Waking the Tiger, North Atlantic Books, 1997

McKnight, John & Peter Block, The Abundant Community, Berret-Koehler, 2010

Macy, Joanna & Chris Johnstone, Active Hope, New World Library, 2012

Marx, Karl Selected Writings, ed. David McLellan, Oxford University Press, 1977

Mertes, Tom, A Movement of Movements, Verso, 2004

Rodney, Walter, How Europe Underdeveloped Africa, Bogle-L'Ouverture, 1972

Schwartz, Glenn M and John J Nichols (eds), After Collapse, University of Arizona Press, 2006

Senge, Peter, Otto Scharmer, Joseph Jaworski& Betty Sue Flowers, Presence, Doubleday, 2004

Sharp, Gene, Waging Nonviolent Struggle, Extending Horizons Books, 2005

Shiva, Vandana, Earth Democracy, Zed Books, 2016

Shrestha, Nandra, In the Name of Development, University Press of America, 1997

Solnit, Rebecca, A Paradise Built in Hell, Penguin Books, 2009

Thunberg, Greta, No One Is Too Small To Make A Difference, Penguin, 2019

Turner, Graham, Is Global Collapse Imminent? MSSI Research paper 4, August 2014

The Trapese Collective, Do It Yourself, a handbook for changing the world, Pluto Press, 2007

Trungpa, Chogyam, Shambhala, The Sacred Path of the Warrior, Shambhala Books, 2007

Wallerstein, Immanuel, Utopistics, The New Press, 1998

Wahl, Daniel, Designing Regenerative Cultures, Triarchy Press, 2016

Wheatley, Margaret, Walk Out, Walk On, Berrett-Koehler Publishers, 2011

Wheatley, Margaret, Who Do We Choose To Be?, Berrett-Koehler Publishing, 2017

Young, Jon, Ellen Haas & Evan McGown, Coyote's Guide, OwlLink Media, 2016

Zunin, Leonard, Contact – The First Four Minutes, Ballantine Books, 1972.

Podcasts –

The following are all available from all good podcast sources:
Charles Eisenstein – The New and Ancient Story
The Hedge School
Bioneers – Revolution From the Heart of Nature

Film

I have found Films For Action to be a wonderful library of diverse documentaries and thought provoking films.

Sources

[i] For an account of the origins of this phrase, made famous by Martin Luther King Jr. go to: https://quoteinvestigator.com/2012/11/15/arc-of-universe/

[ii] Private email correspondence

[iii] Thomas Cleary, The Taoist I Ching, Shambhala Publications, 1986

[iv] Helmut Wilhelm, I Ching, Princeton University Press, 1977

[v] Thomas Cleary, The Taoist I Ching, Shambhala Publications, 1986

[vi] I Ching, Helmut Wilhelm, Princeton University Press, 1977. Jung's Forward written in 1949

[vii] Huai-Chin Nan, Tao and Longevity, Element Books, 1988

[viii] I must credit Charles Eisenstein for the notion of a "new and ancient story" and The More Beautiful World Our Hearts Know is Possible.

[ix] All extracts from the I Ching are taken from Stephen Karcher's interpretation: How to Use the I Ching, A Guide to Working With The Oracle of Change, Element Books, 1997

[x] Margaret Wheatley, Who Do We Choose To Be?, Berrett-Koehler Publishing, 2017

[xi] Gaia in Ancient Greece was the primordial deity, the Goddess of the Earth. Resurrected by James Lovelock, the Gaia Hypothesis maintains that the world is a complex, self-regulating system, a living entity.

[xii] Karl Marx, Preface to a Critique of Political Economy, in Selected Writings, Oxford University Press, 1977

[xiii] Karl Marx, Preface to a Critique of Political Economy, in Selected Writings, Oxford University Press, 1977

[xiv] Jared Diamond, Collapse: How Societies Choose to Fail or Succeed, Penguin, 2011

[xv] Joanna Macy, The Shambhala Warrior, Awaking.org. http://www.awakin.org/read/view.php?tid=236

[xvi] Immanuel Wallerstein, personal email correspondence

[xvii] Dreaming the Council Ways, Ohky Simine Forest, Samuel Weiser, 2000

[xviii] Presencing is a term coined by Otto Scharmer and colleagues of the Presencing Institute. It is the moment of emergence in a change process when actors stop what they're doing to allow the future to show itself, to make itself present.

[xix] I have adopted the term The More Beautiful World from Charles Eisenstein whose book The More Beautiful World Our Hearts Know is Possible has hugely influenced these pages. (North Atlantic Books, 2013.)

[xx] This prophecy is described by Phil Lane Jr. a Chief of the Yankton Dakota and Chickasaw First Nations (US and Canada).
https://www.fwii.net/profiles/blogs/the-prophecy-of-the-reunion-of
[xxi] Collective poems have been composed in various workshops I have facilitated. Participants contribute lines that resonate for them and these are combined into a single poem that conveys a multitude of meanings and intentions.

[xxii] Facebook post

[xxiii] Ugo Bardi, The Limits to Growth Revisited, Springer, 2011.

[xxiv] Is Global Collapse Imminent? Graham Turner, MSSI Research paper 4, August 2014.

[xxv] C Jurs, A Wake-Up Call, 2017, Facebook post retrieved from
https://www.facebook.com/cynthia.jurs/posts/10155756791443466

[xxvi] See for example, Glenn M Schwartz and John J Nichols (eds), After Collapse, University of Arizona Press, 2006

[xxvii] Quoted by Ellen Morris in After Collapse, as above.

[xxviii] Greta Thunberg, No One Is Too Small To Make A Difference, Penguin, 2019

[xxix] Jem Bendell, Deep Adaptation: A Map for Navigating Climate Tragedy, IFLAS Occasional Paper 2, July 27, 2018. https://www.lifeworth.com/deepadaptation.pdf
[xxx] Charles Eisenstein, On Movements and Activism, Jan 8, 2015.
https://www.youtube.com/watch?v=lOowBEsatwQ&list=PLSAXcDj7_tnDvPQxatF6CPiOhMK mbgMzE&t=0s&index=3

[xxxi] Rhonda Fabian, Five Insights about Global Transformation from the Kosmos Study, Connecting Change, Kosmos Journal, Oct 6, 2015. https://www.kosmosjournal.org/news/five-insights-about-global-transformation-from-the-kosmos-study-connecting-for-change/

[xxxii] Carey Clouse, Cuba's Urban Farming Revolution: How to Create Self-Sufficient Cities, The Architectural Review, 17 March 2014. http://www.architectural-review.com/archive/cubas-urban-farming-revolution-how-to-create-self-sufficient-cities/8660204.fullarticle

[xxxiii] Arundhati Roy, Speech to the World Social Forum, 2003

[xxxiv] I have borrowed this phrase from Adebayo Akomolafe who is quoted later in this chapter.

[xxxv] John Dennis Liu and Bradley T Hiller, A Continuing Inquiry into Ecosystem Restoration: Examples from China's Loess Plateau and Locations Worldwide and Their Emerging Implications, Land Restoration: Reclaiming Landscapes for a Sustainable Future, 2016, pages 361-379. http://eempc.org/a-continuing-inquiry-into-ecosystem-restoration/

xxxvi Agenda Gotsch, Life in Syntropy, Dec 2, 2015.
https://www.youtube.com/watch?v=gSPNRu4ZPvE

xxxvii K D Longboat, A Path to Sacred Healing: Answering Humanity's Great Call, 2015. Podcast:
http://indigenouswisdomsummit.com/library/8681/7800

xxxviii Lao Tzu: Tao Te Ching, A New English version by Ursula K Le Guin, Shambhala
Publications, 1998

xxxix Facebook post

xl Jeanne Croteau, How Gardening Can Fight Stress And Improve Your Life, Forbes, Mar 27,
2019. https://www.forbes.com/sites/jeannecroteau/2019/03/27/how-gardening-can-fight-stress-
and-improve-your-life/

xli Vandana Shiva: https://www.facebook.com/playgroundenglish/videos/609794979353836/

xlii Adam Brock, Change Here Now, Chapter 6, North Atlantic Books, 2017

xliii The phrase is attributed to science fiction writer William Gibson.

xliv Leonard Zunin, Contact – The First Four Minutes, Ballantine Books, 1972.

xlv Claude Alvares, My Unlearning Journey: An Interview with Manish Jain, Shikshantar.
http://www.shikshantar.org/articles/my-unlearning-journey-interview-manish-jain

xlvi Charles Eisenstein, Climate – A New Story, North Atlantic Books, 2018.

xlvii Original link: http://siliconafrica.com/the-alternative-to-capitalism/

xlviii The Levellers Standard Advance, 1649,
https://scholarsbank.uoregon.edu/xmlui/bitstream/handle/1794/863/levellers.pdf?sequence=1&is
Allowed=y

xlix Facebook post, 5 January 2019,
https://www.facebook.com/groups/1206960359323785/permalink/2214933825193095/

l Paul Hawken, Blessed Unrest, Penguin, 2007

li Erica Chenowth, The success of nonviolent civil resistance, TEDx Boulder, 2013. https:
//tedxboulder.com/speakers/erica-chenoweth. There are a range of Erica Chenoweth talks on
Youtube.

lii On-line interview: S Van Gelder, Pancho Ramos Stierle: Nonviolence Is Radical, February 23,
2012. Original link: https://www.yesmagazine.org/peace-justice/pancho-ramos-stierle-
nonviolence-is-radical

liii P McCabe, The Hoop of Life, 2017. Facebook post retrieved from:
https://www.facebook.com/pat.mccabe.5454/posts/1735746796455937

liv The Forgiveness Project: Desmond Tutu. https://www.theforgivenessproject.com/desmond-
tutu

lv This can be watched on Youtube: https://www.youtube.com/watch?v=OjotlPIlRqw

[lvi] Native Momma, Churches denounce Doctrine of Discovery, Nov 3, 2016.
https://www.youtube.com/watch?v=q1x6zuYp0g0&t=3s

[lvii] Podcast: https://soundcloud.com/user-657128117/malidoma-some

[lviii] Occupy Movement, The 'Global May manifesto' of the International Occupy assembly,
The Guardian, 11 May 2012.
https://www.theguardian.com/commentisfree/2012/may/11/occupy-globalmay-manifesto

[lix] On-line interview: S Van Gelder, Pancho Ramos Stierle: Nonviolence Is Radical, February 23,
2012. Original link: http://www.yesmagazine.org/peace-justice/pancho-ramos-stierle-
nonviolence-is-radical

[lx] Rudyard Griffiths, Micah White: 'Occupy Wall Street was a constructive failure', The Globe
and Mail, March 18, 2016. https://www.theglobeandmail.com/opinion/munk-debates/micah-
white-occupy-wall-street-was-a-constructive-failure/article29294222/

[lxi] Adam Bucko, Occupy Spirituality, North Atlantic Books, 2013

[lxii] Gene Sharp, Waging Nonviolent Struggle, Extending Horizons Books, 2005

[lxiii] George Lakey, Towards a Living Revolution, Peace News Press, 2012

[lxiv] Lorenz Gramann, I hear A Call, Jul 6, 2017. A video portrayal of this event and its poem:
https://www.youtube.com/watch?v=98zoI2eS6J4&t=3s

[lxv] Commonway: Creating a World that Works for All. Original Link:
http://www.commonway.org/sri_lanka_overview

[lxvi] Sharriff Abdullah, Creating a World That Works for All, Berrett-Kohler Publishers, 1999

[lxvii] Global Gathering for Peace and Healing for Mexico and the World.
http://www.rootlight.com/library/globalgathering.htm

[lxviii] David Nicol, Subtle activism: An idea whose Time has Come, September 15, 2015.
http://subtleactivism.net/subtle-activism-idea-whose-time-has-come/

[lxix] Iulia Leulua, Native Affairs Summer Series – Whanganui river to be recognised as a person, 6
Dec 2016. http://www.maoritelevision.com/news/regional/native-affairs-summer-series-
whanganui-river-be-recognised-person

[lxx] Constitution of the Republic of Ecuador, 2008,
http://pdba.georgetown.edu/Constitutions/Ecuador/english08.html

[lxxi] End Ecocide on Earth, Center for Progressive International Law. https://www.endecocide.org/

[lxxii] Sandra Postel, A River in New Zealand Gets a Legal Voice, National Geographic Society, Sept
4, 2012. http://voices.nationalgeographic.com/2012/09/04/a-river-in-new-zealand-gets-a-legal-
voice/

[lxxiii] Jason Hickel, Enough of aid – let's talk reparations, The Guardian, 27 November 2015. https://www.theguardian.com/global-development-professionals-network/2015/nov/27/enough-of-aid-lets-talk-reparations.

[lxxiv] David Love, Britain Compensated 46,000 Slave Owners But Will Not Pay Slavery Reparations, David Cameron Builds Jamaican Prison Instead, Atlanta Black Star, Sept 30, 2015. https://atlantablackstar.com/2015/09/30/britain-compensated-46000-slave-owners-but-will-not-pay-slavery-reparations-david-cameron-builds-jamaican-prison-instead/?fbclid=IwAR0TbAQhgGTxDbtwRM_8LIGELmekCnYko8JY5KDZ1tRjm4KXxmyfcnEx76c

[lxxv] https://www.facebook.com/groups/1206960359323785/permalink/2583376628348811/

[lxxvi] Youtube video from 23 July 2017, but now private and unavailable. Original link: https://www.youtube.com/watch?v=Bh9UKcJgHY0&t=8116s

[lxxvii] This invocation is an adaptation of the Native Hawaiian ceremony of forgiveness, the Ho'oponopono.

[lxxviii] George Monbiot, The new political story that could change everything, TEDSummit 2019. https://www.ted.com/talks/george_monbiot_the_new_political_story_that_could_change_everything/transcript#t-259042

[lxxix] Rebecca Solnit, A Paradise Built in Hell, Penguin Books, 2009

[lxxx] This story is retold by David Benjamin-Blower in Sympathy For Jonah, 2016. https://benjaminblower.bandcamp.com/merch/sympathy-for-jonah

Other novels, novellas and short story collections available from Stairwell Books

For further information please contact rose@stairwellbooks.com
www.stairwellbooks.co.uk
@stairwellbooks